String Theory

and the

Transparent

Patient

A Novel

By

Wig Nelson

ISBN-13: 978-0-9966487-0-7

XP

Xeries Press
Indialantic, Florida

First Edition July 2015
10 9 8 7 6 5 4 3 2 1 2 3 4 5 6 7 8 9 10

Acknowledgments

Special thanks to Mary Nelson who, when I first show her a new book, always asks me, "Yeah, so now what?"

Also by Wig Nelson

The Psychic

Starry Night

The Conga Player's Dues

Jacks & Hands

The Little Shop of Lyrics

The Oddfellows Home and Other Short Stories

Sirens*

The First Church of Siren*

Online*

*The Sirens Trilogy

String Theory

and the

Transparent

Patient

Chapter One

"My neighbor told me Thursday is his favorite day. It's such a nobody day, isn't it, Dr. Hamm?"

Hamm said nothing. He absentmindedly stroked his wispy goatee beneath his equally wispy mustache. His ex-wife pleaded with him to shave it off but he had grown attached to it since medical school. It was slightly red in color as was his thick copse of brush-cut hair. He looked more like an artist than a psychiatrist and often used his looks to put his patients at ease. His clothes were rather casual as well. He wore khaki slacks with no socks above his scuffed up Docksiders. His shirt was a button-downed, oxford with a wrinkled collar, which spoke to the fact that he was a bachelor and undoubtedly did his own laundry. Jerome, who was sitting on his couch and complaining about Thursday for some reason, was a clean-shaven man in his early thirties. He looked a lot more like he should be the analyst, as he had dark, curly hair and a rather large Roman nose with a small, dark mole on the right side. His shoes were in much better shape as well. He continued his diatribe, "The Japanese attacked Pearl Harbor on a Sunday. Now *that's* a day! Thursday leaves me with a feeling like cold porridge, doesn't it you? Now I suppose I'm speaking out of turn again, aren't I? But it's such an unremarkable name for a day, wouldn't you say, Dr. Hamm?"

Hamm said nothing. He let his patient continue.

"I suppose I should thank you for being my therapist, or analyst or whatever, but I don't really care much about labels and such. And as far as putting words in my mouth, if you want to know what I'm talking about, just ask me for Heaven's sake. What kind of body do I have to leave behind to just make the world quit dogging me?"

"You're sounding very angry, Jerome."

"I haven't slept."

"Since when?"

"Oh, I don't know . . . nineteen . . .?"

"Be serious, Jerome."

"I'll tell you what serious is, Doctor. Serious is what I'm feeling in my chest right now. It is a constriction; kind of like a bout of gas after an episode of acute indigestion, but there is more. There is the certainty that what I'm feeling is around my heart, and in my heart, and that it will probably not last much longer."

"Who is putting words in your mouth? Let's talk about that," said Hamm.

"Oh, I don't know. I just feel like no one takes me seriously."

"Serious as a heart attack. Is that it?" asked the doctor.

"I've heard the expression if that's what you mean."

"You brought it up, Jerome. Do you think there is something wrong with your heart?"

"Probably not," said Jerome.

"What did you mean by leaving a body behind?"

"I guess I meant making a difference."

"A difference, how?"

"You know, being remembered for something. *Doing* something."

"What do you think you should be doing, Jerome?"

"I think that's the problem. I don't know. That is to say, I can't remember what I'm supposed to be doing. I think that's why I'm here."

"You mentioned your neighbor. Where does your neighbor live?"

"Obviously, right next to me," said Jerome irritably.

"What's the address?"

"I don't know."

"But you say it's right next door to you. What is *your* address?"

Jerome began to perspire a bit more heavily, "That's also the problem. I can't remember."

"What does your driver's license say?" asked Hamm.

"I can't find it. I have no ID at all."

"So, I can't expect to be paid, is that it?"

"That's all you doctors care about isn't it? The money."

"If you say so. So, what did your neighbor say to you, Jerome? What else did he say aside from Thursday being his favorite day?"

"He said I am probably as normal as you or he is."

"He might be right."

"For the record, right?"

"What? You think I'm only just covering my ass? I wouldn't want to respond to some kind of tragedy that could have been avoided if you were a little more forthcoming with your next move."

"People don't have this kind of conversation, Doctor. Lawyers and other lawyers do, after the fact."

"I'll tell you right now, Jerome, sick or not, your delusions are mine to put a timely end to. I await the opportunity with relish."

"So, I'm nothing more than a hot dog to you, is that it?"

"That's almost funny, Jerome, but you acting like a juvenile supersedes any kind of humor you might think you could pull off, being the festering dead spirit that you are."

"Don't mince words, sweetheart. Tell me what you *really* think."

"I think that what is wrong with *you* is what will someday be wrong with all of us."

"You see? I'm the same as you, Doctor."

"Not, exactly the same . . . Jerome."

"What are you saying?" he asked miserably.

"You are passed over to the other side."

"What other side?" asked Jerome.

"Death."

"Death," he said obliviously. "I'm dead," he again stated deadpan.

"As a door nail, but I have to admit that I have no idea what that means anymore."

"So, how am I communicating with you?"

"I honestly don't know."

"Very convenient," said Jerome.

"OK, you win. Ignore me, and go on your way to . . . wherever. I'll give you about one second to reconsider it."

"So, what does a dead person do?" asked Jerome.

"Everything that he can," said the doctor.

"So, I guess you couldn't help me, is that right?"

"I'm not sure anyone could have helped you, Jerome."

"Maybe with a few more years of study, you could have helped me. Your residency was what . . . five, six years?" asked Jerome.

"Apparently, not enough, if you are going to judge me to be incompetent."

"What is the alternative, doctor?"

"That you are a twenty-four carat lunatic. Some people are beyond help. They told us that, as well, in residency."

"Good to know."

"So, now you can resume your destiny."

"Which is?"

"A ghost, for lack of a better word."

"Oh, swell. Would you like me to haunt anyone in particular?"

"No, Jerome, just me."

"What makes you say that I'm dead? Are you like that little kid in the movie, who says, *I see dead people*?"

"No, Jerome. I don't see dead people. There *are* no dead people, only dead bodies; corpses, if you will."

"But, you see me."

"Unfortunately, yes, I do."

"So how do you explain it, Doctor?" asked Jerome reaching out to fiddle with the bust of Sigmund Freud sitting on Hamm's desk. His hand passed right through it and appeared again on the other side. Dr. Hamm squinted his already closed eyes in avoidance of the sight. He stroked his beard and said, "Please don't do that, Jerome. It's obscene. I told you no parlor tricks if I'm going to treat you."

7

"Treat me? Isn't it a little late for that?" he asked.

"Whatever. I'll call it whatever you like. Pass over . . . move on . . . what would you have me call it?"

"So, now think you're like that Ghost Whisperer woman. Trust me; you don't have the rack for it."

"No, Jerome. I'm not a Ghost Whisperer. You watched too much television."

"I still watch television, Doctor. I just have a little trouble changing the channel."

"Show me," said Dr. Hamm.

Jerome reached out to the coffee table positioned in front of the soft, black leather couch on which he was sitting. As his hand passed through the remote control, the television in the corner came to life."

"There," he said triumphantly. "That's really something, isn't it?"

"Yes, Jerome. It's a fine parlor trick."

"It's no trick, Doctor Hamm. I did it, and you know it."

"Again, it's nothing I can prove. There can be a timer within the television, which is set to turn itself on at a given time."

"But, you know there isn't."

"Yes, Jerome. I know."

"So, why don't we show your receptionist again?"

"No, Jerome, not again. We tried that, and all she did was lose a little respect for me. After all, she can't see you, can she?"

"Apparently, not."

"Why is that, Jerome?" asked Dr. Hamm. "Why am I the only person you show yourself to?"

"Lucky you, huh?"

"Lucky me."

"Would you like me to leave? Forever?"

"You have no idea how much."

"Do you always give up on your patients so easily?"

"You are not a patient. You're not paying me, Jerome. You're just taking up my time."

"Don't give me that crap. I know how important I am to you. If I'm not real, if I'm not dead and sitting here on your couch, then *you* are a very sick man."

"Now you're doing my job, is that it?"

"I'm just saying . . ."

"There is nothing wrong with my mind, Jerome."

"Then, you have to admit it. I'm dead and in contact with the living. If I'm the first one in history, doesn't that do something for that ginormous ego of yours?"

"My ego is no larger than normal."

"No God complex? What kind of doctor *are* you."

"Obviously, a good one. You chose to come to me. I'm guessing you had your pick of the lot."

"Of, course."

"Why else, me, unless you think I'm the best, Jerome."

"You are a golfer. I saw you play in the Pro-Am at Pebble Beach one year. I play golf as well, hence the connection."

"Just about every psychiatrist is a golfer, Jerome. The game makes us crazy."

"Whatever. Let's just get to it, can we?"

"It's your dime, Jerome."

9

"Try and spend it."

"Call it pro bono."

"I've heard of Sonny Bono . . ."

"Look, Jerome. My day starts in about ten minutes. At that time, I will deal with the living, breathing patients who are trying to become better people. I'm going to deal with people who say real things about real issues and can change the channel if they want to."

"How many psychiatrists does it take to change a light bulb, Dr. Hamm?"

"I've heard it, Jerome," said Hamm in an irritated tone.

"Three, and the light bulb really has to want to change," said Jerome, ignoring the doctor's allusion to his ignominious behavior.

"What you're doing is a crime, Jerome. I know you can't go to jail or anything, but what you are doing is stealing."

"I know. Your valuable time, blah blah blah."

"You're going to have to show me something tangible. By the next time we meet, if you can't show me some proof, then I'm going to conclude that *I'm* the one who needs help. I will seek help from my wife, whom you know is also a very competent analyst, although we no longer reside together. After which time, I will cease to meet with you either in this office or at whatever venue you choose to haunt."

"Haunt is such an ugly word, Dr. Hamm. It reminds me of *Casper the Friendly Ghost*, or worse yet, Thursday."

"Think about it, Jerome. Bring me something I can sink my teeth into or get the hell out, for good."

"You'll get your proof, Doctor."

~

Chapter Two

Shortly after Jerome left his office, Dr. Hamm pressed the intercom button on his desk, "Allison, has my nine o'clock appointment arrived yet?" he released the button and waited for her response. Nothing. He pressed the button again, "Allison, has Mrs. Peters shown up yet? I have ten after nine, and she's usually never late for our sessions." Still, there was nothing from the intercom. Dr. Hamm rose from his chair and walked forcefully to the door to his waiting room. *If Allison is texting again on office time, I'm going to suggest she look elsewhere for . . .* he grabbed the handle and jerked the door open only to find an empty room. Allison's sweater was not on the back of her chair like it usually was, and her purse was not on the floor beside her desk. *Late again for work,* he thought angrily. Then he caught himself failing to practice what he preaches. *Tolerance is the key,* he reminded himself, once again. *Allison probably has a good reason for being late. I'll bet she missed the train again. I can't blame her for not taking a cab with what they charge these days, and the cross-town busses have been murder lately with the construction on forty-Fifth Street.* Suddenly, the outer door to the lobby opened, and rather than Allison, Jerome stormed quickly back into the room, "Dr. Hamm, I'm so glad you haven't left yet."

Left yet? Thought the doctor with a puzzled expression on his face, *I've just arrived to start the day, Jerome. You know that. You've only been gone for about five minutes, Jesus what a situation this is, and I won't take a valium so early in the day. Physician, heal thyself,* thought Hamm.

"I don't have time for this, Jerome. I thought we were clear on that. The living come first."

"Dr. Hamm, you asked for something tangible; you asked for proof, well, I have it for you now."

"We'll have to take this up later, Jerome. I have patients with real issues, and it's my job to take that very seriously."

"Mrs. Peters won't be coming in today," said Jerome flatly.

"What are you talking about, Jerome?"

"Your patient. Judy Peters had a slight fall and bruised her hip. She won't be making her appointment."

"When did this happen?"

"Last night, about ten, but I just saw it recently, in fact, just a moment ago. I don't know how or why this kind of thing is happening, but it's true. You know it's true, right?"

"I don't know anything, Jerome."

"I saw her fall in her house. She lives in Brooklyn, on Elm between Archer and Freeman. Her husband walks with a cane from an old injury he suffered during the first Gulf War. Nineteen ninety-one, shortly after Kuwait fell to Saddam's Guard during the first attack. His Bradley suffered an RPG attack."

"You've been on the internet, is that it, Jerome?"

"Not even close, Dr. Hamm. I saw it all. I don't know how I can look back in time, but what else makes sense."

"Certainly not you," said Hamm.

"So, there's your proof."

"Proof of what?"

"You said you wanted something tangible you could sink your teeth into. Well, sink your teeth into that, Dr. Hamm."

"What you've told me proves nothing. There are any number of ways you could have found out that . . ."

"He hits her."

Dr. Hamm suddenly stopped his retort and said, "What did you say?"

"I said he hits her."

"Who are you talking about, Jerome?" asked the doctor.

"Mrs. Peters' husband, William. He has been hitting her on a regular basis ever since he returned from the Middle East."

"How would you know such a thing?"

"I don't know how, but I do. You asked for proof, and there, I think I've given it to you."

"I don't know what you've given me, but I wouldn't call it proof. Mrs. Peters is a lovely woman who donates a lot of her time to troubled veterans dealing with PTSD. She and her husband both volunteer at the VA clinic down on Fairchild Street. I'm sure that's the connection that you've mistakenly confused with your vision of abuse from William Peters. According to his wife, he is a very peaceful man."

"I'm sure he is, until he hits her. Never in the face; he wouldn't want to leave a mark."

"Look, Jerome, I don't have time for this. I'm going to have to ask you to leave."

13

"Oh, sure, you don't have time. You never have time for me, Dr. Hamm. All you ever do is ask me to leave. You know, you could give a guy a complex with all of your rejection."

"Maybe that's what I have in mind. Call it job security. If I really mess up your mind, I'll have to work with you for a long time."

"Lucky you're not a comedian, Dr. Hamm. You'd starve to death, because you're definitely not funny."

"I'm sorry, Jerome. I suppose that was cruel of me. I promise you we will resume your therapy, but you'll have to leave this office for the time being. I'm running behind, and my receptionist is late again."

"She won't be in either, Dr. Hamm."

"Just what the hell are you talking about, Jerome?"

"Your receptionist, Allison Cole."

"What about Allison? What do you know?"

"She is down in Florida right now, visiting with friends on spring break."

"I don't think so, Jerome."

"They're in Daytona Beach. Give her a call on her cell phone if you don't believe me."

Dr. Hamm picked up the land line on Allison's desk and dialed her cell phone number.

Do to the large volume of cell phone activity, your call cannot be completed at this time, came the recording.

"Well?" asked Jerome.

"The call didn't go through," said Hamm.

"That's because every kid down there in Florida is trying to make a call and cluttering up the airwaves."

"I don't think Florida has anything to do with it, Jerome."

"She's been job hunting lately. She's had three interviews this week."

"Allison is well paid, and I pay for her health insurance as well."

"All the same, don't expect to see her today, Dr. Hamm, or tomorrow either, for that matter."

"Look, Jerome. You do a fine song and dance, but what you have given me is no proof of anything. I asked you for something tangible. You can turn on the television with the remote control, but you can't change the channel or turn up the volume. Until you can do something like that, I don't think I can take this whole affair seriously."

"What do you want me to do?"

"Take my hand, for starters. Let me feel that you have some kind of corporeal presence in the world."

Jerome reached out and tried to grasp the hand of Dr. Hamm. He was unsuccessful. His had passed through the doctor's, resulting in a very unpleasant reaction. Hamm abruptly pulled back his hand and said, "Jesus, that's creepy, Jerome!"

"You're the one who asked me," said Jerome.

"I asked you to take me hand, not reach through it. You can't imagine how disgusting that is."

"It's no bowl of cherries for me either, Dr. Hamm. It's very frustrating. It feels like running in a dream and you never get anywhere. Do you know what I mean?"

"Unfortunately, yes. I know exactly what you mean. Still, that doesn't mean I believe you."

"What's not to believe? I'm here, and I'm not. I can act like I'm alive, but now I know that I'm dead. So, do you. You said so yourself."

"I'm not sure what I believe anymore. But you're making it very hard to believe in you, Jerome."

"I'm working on it. What would convince you that I'm for real . . . err. . . so to speak?"

"Show me something that only a person who has visited the other side can know."

"Like what?" asked Jerome.

"I don't know. Predict the future or something. Tell me tomorrow's lottery numbers."

"I'm not sure it works like that, Dr. Hamm. Nobody can tell the future, alive *or* dead."

"Then, just take my hand, Jerome. When you can take my hand, I'll believe what you say."

~

Chapter Three

As Jerome was just going through the outer door from the lobby to the street, a heavy-set woman seemed to pass right through him on the way in. He noticed a nametag on her blazer which proclaimed, *'Marie Boardman – Century 21 Million Dollar Agent - 2015.'* In tow was a short, bearded, young Hispanic gentleman who wore glasses on a bulbous nose. He seemed to be at the end of his endurance, braving the stifling heat of the humid, August afternoon. When he came through the door, following the stout woman, the cool air from a large register set on the floor was a sorely needed oasis. He was sweating profusely, and his light blue shirt became a darker blue around his armpits and on the front of his torso. After catching his breath, he addressed the woman in front of him, "I appreciate your diligence, Ms. Boardman, and your efforts have been most thorough, however, the last property you showed me will be suitable for my needs. I have a very small practice at this point, and I have to keep my expenses down."

"That's why we're here, Mr. Garcia, please bear with me for just a moment longer."

"As you wish, but I don't think this address is within my means, if you know what I mean."

"This property is in a rent-controlled district, Mr. Garcia. Although it *is* in the heart of downtown, and over thirteen-hundred square feet, the rent is only twenty-three hundred dollars per month.

There are two treatment rooms, with adjoining half-baths, and an outer waiting room with a desk for a receptionist. The file cabinets are built-ins, and the carpet was just replaced recently. There really *is* no better bang for your buck in the area."

"But you said that you are not sure of its availability."

"That is merely a conversation for your benefit alone. This is what we call in the business a *'pocket listing.'* It's really not on the market, but I have it on good authority that it will be very soon."

"Oh, what are the circumstances?" he asked wiping his brow with a handkerchief.

"This unit was the office of a very prominent psychiatrist, for the last twelve years. His patients were exclusively city residents, and he chose to set up shop here to accommodate them."

"That was very kind of him," said Dr. Garcia. "He surely could have kept his overhead down in one of the professional buildings in the boroughs. What was his name?"

"His name was Jerry Hamm. I shouldn't talk about him in the past tense. He is still alive, although just barely. His name *is* Jerry Hamm."

"That is very sad," said Garcia. "What are *his* circumstances, if I might ask?"

"He was in a terrible accident about ten days ago. The cab he was riding in was t-boned on Columbus Avenue during rush hour. They had to cut him out of the car with the *Jaws of Life*."

"How unfortunate," said Garcia. "I will say a prayer for him and his family."

"He is alone, as I understand it. He has no family, but a wife who has left him, of late."

"So sad to die alone."

"He's not dead yet. He has been in a coma since the accident, and he's lying in the ICU ward at Mercy Hospital down on Fulton. He hasn't regained consciousness since the accident."

"Well, I hope that he returns to this office and resumes his practice."

"I do, as well, Dr. Garcia. But just in case this comes available, I wanted you to see it."

"Thank you, Ms. Boardman. Your job, it would seem, is an unpleasant one, dealing with the hardship of others."

"Life goes on, Dr. Garcia. Life goes on."

~

Fulton Street, thought Jerome. *Mercy Hospital was only thirteen blocks away; four over to Sixth, and then nine down to Fulton. He could easily walk there in under an hour. Could it be true that Dr. Hamm was in their ICU? Had he really been there for the last ten days?* It seemed impossible to Jerome. He had met with the doctor on three occasions in the last week. True, their sessions were brief, and he was not actually on the doctor's schedule, but he had accommodated him just the same. He was a good man. Jerome had a great deal of respect for Dr. Hamm. He started out at once.

Walking through the city was always unsettling to Jerome. He wasn't a coward, but he had a very good imagination. He knew that, on any given street corner, there were minions of the dark forces peddling drugs who might mistakenly find him in their crosshairs. Children were playing in the streets, and that only made it more pathetic. They were the oblivious, possibly future, statistics who just happened to be in the wrong place at the wrong time. Jerome made sure he would never be among their number. Caution ruled his life, and yet, when he thought of Dr. Hamm lying in a hospital bed, less than half-a-mile away, he scolded himself for his hesitation. He knew that his place was by the doctor's side. Not that he could help him in any way, he wasn't a medical man, but he was in tune with the other side. Perhaps he could offer something outside the reach of modern medicine. At any rate, he had no choice but to try. He passed the masses of humanity on the street with a concerted obliviousness born of a city kid, which he had no right to display. He stepped over the homeless and gave the appropriate finger to all the bothersome guerilla panhandlers, forceful though they were. He became one with the dark forces of the city, intent on a mission that was not to be interrupted. When the hospital came into view, he stopped to catch his breath. He stopped also to construct a plan. He couldn't very well barge into the ICU of a major hospital and demand to see a patient who was no relation to him. But, then again, he knew he was less than corporeal. He knew in the deepest part of his heart that he could act as he willed, with no interruption from the personnel of the hospital. He might turn on their television sets inadvertently, but that would probably be the most of his evident presence. He had a duty to his doctor; to see if he needed anything from his latest, albeit unwelcome, transparent patient. He passed through the front entrance of the hospital and didn't bother to stop at the desk where the visitor passes were issued. No one would observe his passage through the hallways, or his subsequent arrival at the ICU ward, where his doctor was being cared for. It was short work finding the appropriate room. There were ten patients, all in a circular array of curtained-off gurneys, each with tubes coming out of the wall behind them and serving the various needs of their attendants. It seemed that Dr. Hamm was only encumbered by a slim oxygen tube extended into his nostrils. He had an IV attached to his arm, displaying the title of D5L Lactated Ringers, which somehow Jerome knew to be merely sugar water to keep the doctor hydrated. He slowly approached the bed.

The rise and fall of Dr. Hamm's chest indicated that he was in a deep sleep, possibly facilitated by a sedative introduced into his IV port as well. He seemed at peace, and Jerome was, all at once, hesitant to disturb him. But he knew that he was there for a reason. Aside from the fact that he needed help from the doctor, he was not there for selfish reasons whatsoever. For once in his life, Jerome was directed into action that was entirely without question. He reached forward and grasped the hand of the doctor. At first, he was disappointed by the cold hand he held in his, and then he realized that the hand had significant substance. His hand didn't pass through the hand of the doctor as it had earlier on that very morning. He felt firm, although alarmingly cold, flesh. A tear came to Jerome's eye as he looked down at the sedentary figure on the bed. And then, he noticed something else. Something wonderful! As he looked down at Dr. Hamm, he noticed a tear on his face, as well. His eyelids began to flutter, and then rising out of a dreamy sleep, the doctor said to him, "Ahh, my proof at last."

~

Chapter Four

The ICU nurse, Bonnie Waters, noticed Jerome standing next to Hamm's bed and immediately walked over to confront him, "Excuse me, sir, this is not a patient room. There are no visitors allowed here. You are in the intensive care unit."

"So, you can see me," said Jerome needlessly.

"Of course, I can see you. What kind of a question is that?"

"I'm sorry, I'm just a little confused . . ."

"You're going to have to leave this room immediately."

"Yes, ma'am, I know that."

"Dr. Hamm is gravely ill."

"I know that, too," said Jerome, "but did you know that Dr. Hamm is no longer in a coma? He just opened his eyes and spoke to me."

"What did you say?" asked Nurse Waters.

"He's awake. He spoke to me."

"Dear, God," said Waters reaching to her collar to trigger an intercom link to the ward desk. "This is Bonnie in ICU, Linda. Please page Dr. Collins ask him to come to the ward. If there's no response, dial his pager and whoever is on call for him. Dr. Hamm has woken up. EEG shows definite brain activity."

Nurse Waters then again spoke to Jerome, "Now, please leave, sir, or I'm going to have to call security."

"I'm going, now, ma'am. I wasn't trying to make any trouble. I'm one of Dr. Hamm's patients," he lied reaching out to shake her hand. When Nurse Waters' hand grasped his lightly, Jerome was relieved to be able to feel her warm flesh in his. *He had substance!* He turned to Dr. Hamm, who was lying with his eyes closed again and said, "Good-bye, Doctor. I'll come back and visit you when you are checked into a room."

"Yes, very well," said Waters, "now leave."

"Thank you nurse," said Jerome on his way out the double swinging doors to the ICU. He had a huge grin on his face. He had substance! He was real! He had a life, even though he couldn't, at present, recall what it entailed. Perhaps it would come back to him soon, just as consciousness had returned to Dr. Hamm. He walked out into the warm, August, noon-day sun and began searching for his identity.

~

Jerome hailed a cab that had a broken, right tail-light. He got in and then suddenly remembered he had no money to pay for it. He quickly told the cabbie, "Pull over, I made a mistake. I . . . 'err forgot my wallet. Let me out here and I'll mail you the fare to this point."

"Just where were you trying to go?" asked the cabbie. He was a short man in his late twenties with and an olive skin tone and dark, straight, hair thinning at the top. His mustache reminded Jerome of Cheech Marin when he was working with Tommy Chong in the seventies. He had kind eyes and a warm smile.

"I'm not really sure," said Jerome. "I have this problem, but it's not your problem. Just let me out here, please."

"Now, wait a minute," said the cabbie. "Just calm down a minute. I'm not going to have you arrested or anything. Give me a chance to help you out. Where is your wallet?"

"I may not have one," said Jerome.

"What?"

"My wallet isn't anywhere that I know of, because I guess I have amnesia."

"Swell," said the hack laconically. "You were right, you're not my problem. You can get out here, forget the fare," he said pulling over to the curb.

"Look, I'm not a deadbeat or anything; at least I don't think I am. I'm just a little confused."

"Uh, huh," said the cabbie, "out, please."

"No, wait, maybe you can help me," said Jerome.

"I'm not a doctor, I just drive a cab."

"I have a doctor. He's at Mercy Hospital on Fulton Street."

"So, that's where you want to go?" asked the cabbie.

"No, I just came from there. He's in ICU. I can't visit him until he gets admitted to a room."

"Uh huh," said the cabbie, "out, please."

"I'm good for the fare, God dammit. Start the meter again," said Jerome.

"Without your wallet," said the cabbie deadpan.

"I mean I will be good for it. I'm *somebody* for God's sake. Look how I'm dressed. These are two-hundred dollar shoes."

"I can't see your shoes, mister. Why don't you just find a nice park bench and sit for a while until you figure things out."

"Can I at least tell you my story?"

"I guess it's lunch time," said the cabbie with a tinge of exasperation in his voice. "How about the Carnegie Deli? We're near Seventh."

"I told you I don't have any money," said Jerome.

"It's my lucky day," said the cabbie.

"I swear I'll pay you back."

"Uh huh," said the cabbie.

~

They had no chance for a parking space around The Carnegie Deli, so the cabbie peeled off a twenty from a roll of bills and said, "I'll buy; you fly. I want a small pastrami on rye with swiss and a little Dijon mustard. Pickle on the side. You want a small, whatever, and I'll meet you back here in about twenty minutes."

"OK, thanks," said Jerome. He took the twenty and left the cab just outside the deli. He searched all the faces he met hoping to find someone familiar to him and got the same, silent response from all of them, *what the hell you lookin' at?* He was elated that Dr. Hamm had regained consciousness and couldn't wait to visit him again when he was allowed to do so. The doctor would be able to give him some clues about his identity, because he distinctly remembered having at least three, albeit, short sessions in his office in the past week. He couldn't really recall them, but he knew that the doctor was likely to, and possibly even had them on a recording that he made clandestinely during his office hours. No one seemed to strike a familiar chord. They all became the faceless masses, as he himself seemed to be. No one cared to look at him or acknowledge his existence. He was once again invisible, although this time, the man behind the lunch counter could actually see him.

~

When the cabbie rounded the block and searched the sidewalk twenty minutes later, Jerome was standing on the curb holding out the bag with his sandwich. He pulled over, and Jerome got in the front seat instead of the back this time. The cabbie said, "Nobody rides up front, pal. Take it to the back seat."

"OK, no problem," said Jerome. "I just thought that I could ride up front here until I could give you your sandwich."

"Back," said the cabbie.

"Alright, I'm going. By the way, what's your name?" asked Jerome.

"You can call me, Kamal."

"Kamal, huh? What is that Greek?" asked Jerome.

"That's right. And your name is. . . ?"

"I'm Jerome. If I knew my last name, I would tell you, but I don't really have a clue."

"You don't know your name?"

"Not really," said Jerome opening the door to get in the back seat.

"So, let me guess. That's your problem right? Amnesia," said Kamal laconically. He acted like he had seen it all driving a hack in New York City and that nothing was ever new to him.

"I know how it sounds, and I never would have thought it could happen to me, but there it is. I guess no one ever thinks it will happen to them until it does."

"So, what's your plan?" asked Kamal.

"The doctor who just came out of the coma at Mercy Hospital. I'm thinking that I mentioned my name to him sometime in the last week."

"That's a pretty thin plan if you ask me. Why not go to the cops and get your prints checked?"

"They do that for free?" he asked.

"How the hell should I know?" said Kamal. "I try to avoid the cops whenever I can. I just figured if you haven't committed any crime in the last few months, you can be safe asking them to run a check on your fingerprints."

"What if I have committed a crime? What if that's why I lost my memory; because I'm suppressing the unpleasant circumstances of it?"

"You're making me lose my appetite, Jerome. Was there any change from the twenty?" asked Kamal.

"No," Jerome lied. He had pocketed the nine dollars change and didn't order a sandwich for himself. He had no desire to eat in the last few days. Maybe it was because he was worried about who he was and possibly what trouble he was avoiding.

"I just had another thought," said Kamal. "They have this new thing called face recognition technology where they can identify a guy by his face. I'm not sure where I heard about it, or who is doing it, but it's worth a shot. In either case, what you want are the cops, not some cabbie."

"What I want is for Dr. Hamm to get checked into a room. That would be a good head start."

"Suit yourself. So, you don't have a sandwich, because you just wolfed it down, right?" asked Kamal questioningly, "and you don't have anywhere to go except back to the hospital on Fulton, right?"

"I guess so," said Jerome.

"So that's where I'm going to take you."

"I'll pay you for your time, Kamal. As soon as I can figure out what's going on."

"Uh huh," said Kamal.

"I just thought you'd like to hear my story."

"I just heard your story, Jerome. You've got amnesia. Big whoopee, so do a lot of guys."

"That's not the whole story, Kamal."

"OK, What else?"

"I think I might be dead or something."

"That's it, get out."

"No, wait a minute. Let me just explain."

"I don't think so," said Kamal. "I don't need any of this shit."

"I used to pass right through things and couldn't touch anything."

"Out," said Kamal.

"OK, I'm going. Jesus, you'd think that I could just catch a break once in a while. Now you've turned your back on me. I guess it just wasn't meant to be."

When Kamal turned around to look in the back seat of the cab, it was empty. Jerome couldn't have gotten out that quickly, and Kamal was shaken to the core. He got out of the cab and looked up and down the sidewalk. He could see no one who looked even remotely like Jerome. At that point, he didn't know what to think. He got back in the front seat of his cab and curled up the top of the bag with his sandwich in it. He had suddenly lost his appetite.

"Kamal, can't you see me?" cried Jerome from the back seat. "I'm right here," he almost yelled. "Oh my God, Dr. Hamm must have fallen back into the coma."

Kamal said nothing.

"You can't hear me?" asked Jerome frantically. "Jesus, at least Dr. Hamm could hear me. Kamal! Answer me," cried Jerome urgently.

Kamal said nothing.

"God dammit," said Jerome. "Alright, I know what I have to do. I'm getting out here, but I'll be back, Kamal. You can't give up on me, dammit! I'm real and I'll prove it to you."

Kamal had decided to end his shift early. He got out of the cab again and opened the back door. He placed his hand inside and felt the seat. It was somewhat warm to the touch, although there was no sign of Jerome. There was instead nine dollars sitting there folded over like they were recently in someone's pocket. He wanted to just go home and lie down for awhile.

Jerome squeezed past him and took off on foot for Mercy Hospital on Fulton Street.

~

Chapter Five

Jerome again found himself at the bedside of Dr. Hamm within the Intensive Care Unit at Mercy Hospital. Dr. Hamm had his eyes closed and Jerome noticed the addition of an EEG monitor as well as the EKG he took note of on his first visit. His oxygen tube was still affixed to his nostrils and a second IV port was connected to the back of his right hand. There were no nurses or other hospital personnel present although Jerome knew that he was beyond their detection in his present state. He reached out and gently took Dr. Hamm by the hand. Again, his eyes began to flutter open at Jerome's touch. He tried to speak out, but his dry raspy throat was unable to make a sound at first. Jerome knew it was only a matter of time before the nurse's station would notice the change in his monitors. He tried to get the doctor's attention and tell him of his experience in the taxi with Kamal.

"Dr. Hamm," he began, "It's Jerome from your office. Do you remember me?"

"Yes," said Hamm weakly.

"You have to stay with us, Dr. Hamm. Try to stay awake. The last time you went back to sleep, my existence was cancelled out again somehow. Do you think you can stay awake?" he asked him.

"I'll try, Jerome."

"Then you remember me. You called me Jerome. Do you remember my last name?"

31

"Cleveland," said Dr. Hamm.

"What about Cleveland, Dr. Hamm? You mean the city?"

"No, Jerome. That is the name you gave me when we first began therapy. You called yourself Jerome Cleveland."

"Then I *am* your patient," said Jerome.

"That's right, you are."

"For how long?" asked Jerome.

"About nine weeks, now," said Hamm.

"But you told me I wasn't your patient. You accused me of wasting your time, remember?"

"No, Jerome. I don't."

"Just yesterday, in your office . . . when your secretary didn't show up for work, remember?"

"I haven't been in my office for two weeks, Jerome. Not since we met just before the consortium at the planetarium."

"What consortium?" asked Jerome, "what planetarium?"

"There was a breakthrough, Jerome. *Your* breakthrough. The fermions and bosons finally mirrored each other outside the collider. You didn't need the hadrons for the attraction after all. You claimed to have the particles of super symmetry contained in a glass vacuum rectangle. Something about keeping the branes on separate planes."

"You mean human brains?" asked Jerome.

"B R A N E S, Jerome, there is no I in branes."

"I don't understand, Dr. Hamm. It's all just a jumbled mess in my mind."

"I think that's why you came to me in the first place, Jerome. You said that your grasp of reality was slipping into another set of strings. You tried to explain it to me, but I remain in the dark," he said sleepily. "I have to rest now, Jerome."

Jerome heard a faint beeping sound coming from Dr. Hamm's EEG monitor. He was sure that the nurse's station was being alerted to his altered state of awareness. He quickly left the doctor's bedside and made his way to the exit before the responding nurse could see him. When he reached the service elevator, he was confronted by two members of the housekeeping staff. He pretended to be lost. After following their directions to the patient floor elevators, he made his way down to the lobby and sat down in one of the chairs by the admission desk. He picked up a magazine and began to pretend he was reading it. His mind was spinning. He wanted to go back and talk to Dr. Hamm in the ICU, but he knew that security would soon escort him to the exit if he tried. He thought his best course of action, or inaction as the case may be, was to kill time. After about twenty minutes, he picked up a house phone next to the admission desk and dialed the extension for patient information. The operator told him that Dr. Hamm was not admitted to a room at this time and to check back later. He made his way to the cafeteria and looked longingly at all the food being kept warm in the trays. He had no money because he somehow left the nine dollars back in Kamal's taxi. He thought that the feeling in his gut was finally hunger pangs and wondered how he could get some food in him. Perhaps he could pretend he was visiting a room and steal one of the patient meals from the dietician's cart. At least he had some more information to go on now. He now knew that his last name was Cleveland. *Jerome Cleveland* he thought. The name didn't ring any bells. It was merely one more piece of the puzzle that his life had become. He decided to leave the hospital for the time being and seek out Kamal's taxi. He went back to the Carnegie Deli with the hope that perhaps Kamal would look there for him after they became separated. But he knew that he had become invisible. He could see that Kamal was visibly shaken by his abrupt departure. He knew he had to tread lightly where Kamal was concerned. He needed a friend in order to get around in the city, and at first, Kamal seemed to want to help him. He hoped that his disappearing act didn't burn any bridges where Kamal was concerned. Especially since now he had a name. His name was Jerome Cleveland. *Who was, or is, Jerome Cleveland?* It was a place to start. He considered finding an old Manhattan phone book and looking under the name Jerome Cleveland, but that was sure to be too tedious a task. There were certainly over a thousand Jerome Clevelands or J. Clevelands in and around Manhattan. *Where to start? What to do? Perhaps the police was a reasonable place to start.*

~

Naturally, the Carnegie Deli was a dead end. That was a long shot at best, so he was not surprised that an hour standing on the corner of Seventh Avenue brought only indifference from the passersby and some hard looks from the panhandlers who claimed the spot as their territory. He decided to walk downtown to Times Square. There was a miniscule precinct of the N.Y.P.D. manned by a two-person team of New York's finest. The woman had sergeant's stripes on her tight-fitting uniform blouse, and Jerome made a concerted effort to keep his eyes above her badge at all costs. She seemed to be a caring individual, a veritable breath of fresh air in a city where none was to be found, when she asked, "How can I help you sir?"

"I seem to be lost, ma'am," said Jerome.

"It's a big city," she said.

"No, it's more than that. I've lost more than my way, Sergeant. I'm not sure that I have a way to begin with."

"Perhaps you could begin at the beginning," she suggested.

Jerome decided to *'cast his fate to the wind,'* so to speak, "I have lost my memory, ma'am," he began, "I can't remember how I got here and what I'm supposed to be doing with my life."

The sergeant looked over to her counterpart and gave a non-visual signal, which surely was the equivalent to rolling her eyes. She said to Jerome, "If I had a nickel for every day someone told me that, I'd be a rich woman." Her partner started to snicker.

"I'm sorry I bothered you, ma'am," said Jerome, "Just forget it." He started to walk away. The sergeant found some sympathy from some deeply stored-away corner of her finely-honed, cynicism and stopped him with her words, "Hey, chill out, mister. I was only messing with you, don't leave, we're here to help. Let's start with your name. Do you remember your name?" she asked him.

"It's Jerome Cleveland," he said.

"Is that a fact?" she asked sardonically. "Well, did you know that I am Albert Einstein in drag?" she asked him raising her eyebrows.

"I remember who Albert Einstein is, or rather was," said Jerome. "I knew this was a bad idea to begin with. Have a nice day, Sergeant," he said making his way to the doorway that opened to a small triangle of raised concrete at the corner of 42nd Street and Eight Avenue. As he was walking through the door, he heard the sergeant's partner say, "I guess he shaved his beard." They both started laughing. When he looked up at the huge electronic billboard suddenly above his head, he saw it. There among a half-million flickering pixels of light was the image of his face. Underneath the picture of the bearded man with glasses flashed the headline: Mysterious Disappearance of Famed Physicist Stumps All Efforts at Traffic Accident Scene! Jerome Cleveland Still Missing!

Jerome fell to his knees. *Physicist? Famed Physicist? Was that possible?* he asked himself. The next thing that Jerome did was steal a newspaper.

~

Chapter Six

Jerome tightly gripped the newspaper he absconded with hastily from a kiosk on Eight Avenue. It had been a sixteen-block trek up from Times Square to 59th Street, but his mind was spinning from the shock of seeing his face on the huge electronic billboard, and he hardly noticed the passage of time. He found an empty park bench at Columbus Circle and sat down to read.

ASSOCIATED PRESS: NEW YORK CITY – *Renowned theoretical physicist Jerome A. (aron) Cleveland remains missing from a severe automobile accident, which occurred eleven days ago at the corner of W 76th Street and Columbus Avenue. He was accompanied by his physician, Dr. Gerald R. Hamm, a prominent psychiatrist with a mid-town Manhattan practice when the accident occurred. The two had just attended a consortium of notable physicists, which were meeting at the Hayden Planetarium on 82nd Street, just a few blocks away. The taxi cab they were riding in was struck violently from the side by another taxi, which was attempting to run a red light. After the accident, Dr. Hamm was stabilized at the scene and then transported to the ICU unit at Mercy Hospital on Fulton Street. Mysteriously, there was no sign of Jerome Cleveland, nor any evidence that he had ever been accompanying Dr. Hamm in the cab. The driver of the stricken vehicle testified to the fact that Cleveland was riding in the rear seat with Dr. Hamm when the accident took place. Also missing from the scene are two articles of luggage belonging to Cleveland that were placed in the trunk of the cab. All efforts to ascertain the whereabouts of Professor Cleveland have to this date remained fruitless. Due to the violent nature of the accident, there is little chance that Dr. Cleveland could have walked away from the scene. So far there is no evidence of foul play, although the FBI has been alerted to a possible kidnapping and is investigating all aspects of the disappearance. Anyone with information regarding this incident is encouraged to notify the local FBI office at 212-555-7500.*

Jerome read the article three times before discarding the paper in the nearest trash receptacle. *Why have I no recollection of the accident? Why don't I have any injuries? Why don't I remember being with Dr. Hamm at the consortium? Why is Hamm my physician? Have I been undergoing analysis? What for?* And most important of all: *What was in the damn trunk of the taxi? Could it have been a glass, rectangular box? I wonder what happens when an isolated group of bosons meet up with their corresponding fermions?*

~

Jerome decided to visit the scene of the accident. He now had a location due to the Associated Press article he had just read. West 76th Street was only seventeen blocks north, and Columbus Avenue was only a block or so west just beyond the convergence of Broadway and Eight Avenue. His mind was divided between wanting to view the scene and for some unknown reason fearing what he might find.

38

The accident was almost two weeks ago and all the signs of the collision would surely be cleaned up by now. But he found himself perspiring as he came further north that had little to do with the August heat of the misty morning. Just as he somehow suspected what he might find, his worst fear was suddenly realized. He could see the body clearly from a block away. It was still lying on the sidewalk, apparently having been thrown from the vehicle. A state of decay was evident by the carrion in attendance. Left to their own devices, the decomposers were free to do their ghastly task, ripping flesh and fighting over any remaining bits of Jerome Cleveland in this isolated dimension of strings vibrating and attached to this particular brane. Aside from the vultures, wild dogs and rats were also well engaged in the fray. Then he noticed the box. It was a small and rectangular; made of glass, and it glowed with an eerie light of its own just a few feet away from the body. Dr. Hamm had mentioned something about the box containing a vacuum. A slight crack in the top sheet of glass spoke to the fact that was no longer the case. The particles within were no longer in a vacuum. He wasn't a big believer in coincidence. He was sure that the damage to the box was the reason for his slipping from one dimension to another. He reasoned that if the box could be repaired, and the particles could be returned to a sealed, static environment, he could maintain his erstwhile unstable position in space and time. How he knew this was a mystery to him. Apparently, his intellect, as well as his memory did not make the transfer between dimensions. Rather than knowledge, it was atavism more than anything that unfolded the certainty of his situation. Along with that atavistic awareness, came the sad conclusion that he was helpless to alter the physical properties of the dimension which held the box. Somehow, Jerome knew he could not retrieve it just as surely as he knew his efforts to chase away the carrion would bear no fruit. A part of his mind was absolutely sure his hand would pass right through the box, and a kick from his two-hundred-dollar shoes would pass harmlessly through the vultures and the dogs and the rats. Jerome found that he was no longer hungry.

~

He made his way back east to Central Park West and turned south toward Columbus Circle. When he reached Central Park South, he turned left and walked along the entrance to the park over to Seventh Avenue. There he turned right and walked four blocks south down to 55th Street where he came across the bustling entrance to the Carnegie Deli. There was a taxi with a broken, right tail-light parked at the curb. He noticed that the light on top was not lit, indicating that the cabbie was off duty. He walked up to the driver's side window and spoke through the glass, "Please, give me a chance to explain, Kamal."

The driver started the engine and pulled away from the curb. Jerome slapped the trunk as it pulled away shouting, "Please, come back, Kamal! I need you. You're probably the only one who can help me now!"

The cab continued down Seventh Avenue and was quickly lost in the throng of jostling, mid-town machines. Jerome stepped up on the curb and searched the immediate area for any sign of a bank.

Now that he knew who he was, he decided to find out just how much money he had. He hoped it was enough.

~

He spotted an ATM on the corner with the Bank of America logo on the top. He had no card to insert nor did he know any pin numbers to use if he had one. Then he noticed a single glass door next to the machine with the B of A logo etched into the surface. He tried the handle and the door swung open. Inside was a staircase leading up to another glass door at the top. He climbed up to the second floor and tried the door. It was locked. Then he noticed the office hours posted on the door. They read: Monday thru Friday 9:00 AM to 12:00 noon – 1:00 PM to 5:00 PM. Closed on Weekends. He didn't know what the time was, but he was sure it was sometime during their lunch hour. He decided to wait it out on the sidewalk below. When he saw the time through the window of the Carnegie Deli, he knew that the bank personnel would be returning shortly. He stood by the door and waited. After a few minutes, two shapely, young women dressed in identical blue, pin striped blazers over ivory colored skirts walked up and opened the door. He asked them, "Do you work at the bank?"

The tallest of the two women answered him, "That's right, sir. Do you have an account here?"

"No," said Jerome.

"Then, are you looking for a cash advance with one of your credit cards?"

"No," said Jerome. "I'd like to open an account."

"I'm sorry," said the woman. "This is not a full service branch. You can open an account at our 34th Street branch. It's located right next to Macy's."

Jerome decided to go for broke with the truth. "I lied to you, Miss. I don't really want to open an account. I have no ID. And what's worse, I have amnesia and I don't know where to turn or what to do. Can you help me, please?"

The woman made eye contact with her partner who continued up the stairs. She turned back to Jerome and said, "Certainly, sir. Just wait here for a moment." She turned and began climbing the staircase following her associate. Jerome saw her speaking into her cell phone and clearly heard the word *'security.'* Realizing what was happening; he turned and bolted for the door leading outside to the street. He could see a man coming down the stairs speaking into a head set and holding a set of keys in his left hand. He reached the bottom and locked the door leading outside the building. He then drew his gun and assumed a *'shooter's stance'* pointing at Jerome's mid-section through the glass door. Jerome turned and ran a block south, looking back over his shoulder every few seconds on the way. He didn't see anyone following him, but he knew it would only be a short time before a member of the local police force would respond. Just as he was about to cross the street, a taxi pulled abruptly up with a short screech of tires and the passenger door flew open. "Get in!" yelled Kamal from the driver's side. "Make it fast Jerome, and you better not have robbed that bank."

Jerome quickly got into the cab and slammed the door shut. Kamal burned a little rubber pulling away from the intersection. He turned to Jerome and said, "I came back because I have to know how you did it."

"Did what?" asked Jerome.

"The disappearing act yesterday. How did you vanish from the back seat of my cab?"

"I'm not sure, but I have an idea. It has to do with particle physics."

"Who do I look like, Stephen Hawking?" asked Kamal facetiously.

"Look, I don't understand it either, but Dr. Hamm said it has something to do with a glass rectangular box that's at the corner of W 76th Street and Columbus Avenue."

"Have you been there, Jerome?"

"Yes."

"And?" asked Kamal.

"The box is there along with . . . a body. I think it might be *my* body."

"You're doing it again, Jerome."

"Doing what?"

"Freaking me out. You're *creeping* me out, and the last time you did it I had to lay down in a dark room for a few hours. Just what the fuck are you talking about?"

"I'm talking about different dimensions. Parallel universes, maybe."

"There's no such thing, Jerome."

"I thought so, too. But now I'm not so sure."

"Start at the beginning, and this time I'm not buying lunch."

"But I'm starving, Kamal."

"Oh, alright. But we have to go downtown a ways. The area around the Carnegie is kind of hot right now because of you."

"I'm sorry."

"Save it. Just start telling me what's going on while I drive."

~

Jerome began telling his story about how he imagined his therapy sessions in Dr. Hamm's office during the last week and how he overheard the Realtor showing the building to a prospective tenant because the present one was near death. He related his experience in the ICU unit of Mercy Hospital and how he shifted between dimensions when Hamm went into and out of a coma. He told Kamal that he didn't understand anything about parallel universes or string theory, but that he saw his likeness on the electronic billboard at Times Square. Kamal headed his taxi there at once. There was no place to park, so he circled the block from Eight Avenue over to Seventh and down to 40th Street and back around. They saw Jerome's face on the billboard on their third trip. Kamal said to him, "It kind of looks like you, but the guy has a beard and glasses."

"I know, but I just have this feeling that it's me. Nothing else makes any sense."

"Your story doesn't make any sense either, Jerome. How is your eyesight? Do you wear glasses? Can you read the small print on the signs?"

"No, I don't need glasses. I can see fine."

"Well, how do you explain the guy on the billboard wearing them? And what about the beard?"

"I guess they just didn't make the transfer."

"What transfer, Jerome?"

"My memory didn't make it either. When I got transferred to this dimension of strings or whatever, my memory didn't come with me. Neither did my beard or my need to wear glasses. And if I'm some kind of theoretical physicist, my intellect didn't make it over here either."

"You can say that again," said Kamal.

"Thanks a lot. You could be a little more supportive, Kamal."

"Since I'm about to buy you lunch again, I'd call that being very supportive, Jerome."

"I said I'll pay you back. For everything, Kamal."

"Sure," said Kamal, "right after you rob another bank."

"Nobody robbed any bank."

"Why were you running?" asked Kamal.

"They were calling the cops."

"Which is what I told you to do yesterday, Jerome."

"I went to the cops right here in Times Square."

"And what did they say?"

"They just made fun of me."

"Because they didn't *believe* you, Jerome. You have to get some kind of proof."

"Here we go again with the proof. Are we going to get something to eat?"

"Yes, we are. And once again it's on my dime. At least I got the nine bucks back that you pocketed."

"What do you mean?" asked Jerome.

"Come on," said Kamal, "it doesn't take a particle physicist to figure it out. My sandwich was ten bucks and change, which you left in the tip jar and that left nine bucks that you pocketed."

"Just what the hell does a particle physicist do, anyway?" asked Jerome.

"Fuck if I know," said Kamal. "Probably looks at a bunch of small shit all day."

"God, I hope that's not what I do for a living. How boring is that?"

"It might be tedious, Jerome, but considering all the shit that's happening to you right now, it sure ain't boring."

~

Chapter Seven

After they grabbed a quick bite to eat at a drive-through, burger chain window, Jerome asked Kamal to return to the scene of the accident and the location of the glass box. When they arrived, Kamal pulled the car over and killed the engine. He turned to Jerome and said, "Now what?"

"You don't see it, do you?"

"See what, Jerome?"

"The body, or rather the buzzards and the bones. That's about all that's left."

"Are you telling me you can see your own dead body?"

"I don't know whose body it is, Kamal. But considering all the facts laid out by the newspaper and Dr. Hamm . . ."

"So, again. Now what?"

"I should try to do something about it."

"Like what?"

"I don't know . . . maybe I should find a way to bury it."

"That's a noble thought, Jerome, but I'm sure it's quite impossible."

"I have to try."

"OK, go ahead. I'll wait here until you're done."

"You could help."

"I don't think so, Jerome. I can't even see it in the first place. How the hell am I going to help you bury it? Besides, it's not even connected to the same brane that we are. You can't dig a hole in another dimension. I can't believe I just said that," said Kamal shaking his head. "Jesus, I'm starting to talk like you."

"Alright, just wait here, and don't leave me."

"Where would I go? It's not like I have a job or anything, like *DRIVING A CAB FOR GOD'S SAKE!*" he yelled after him.

Jerome approached the torn remainder of the body on the sidewalk. The people passing by were understandably oblivious as they no doubt were unable to see into the parallel existence that he could. He didn't understand how he could see it in the first place. Perhaps because his life force once occupied the body, he was connected cosmically for a short while before the spirit left behind ascended to wherever it was destined to go. He didn't feel very comfortable considering the implications. It would have been nice to have a history to reflect upon, something to help him reserve a kind of judgment about the kind of man he had been during his life, but that was just as illusive and transparent as his lost intellect. He kneeled down beside the body and was grateful that his eyesight was the only sense that could transcend the boundaries of his now unstable universe. He imagined that the smell was something out of hell itself. He hoped that his mind's connection to that awful word was where it would come to an end. He wondered if he were a religious man. He began to pray nonetheless amid tears falling on his cheeks. After a few minutes, he returned to Kamal in the taxi. When he opened the rear driver's-side door, Kamal said, "You can ride up front, Jerome. C'mon, get in." Kamal noticed the tears and said, "Man, that couldn't have been easy."

Jerome said nothing. Kamal pulled away from the curb and drove. After a full five minutes of silence, Kamal said, "What about the box?"

"It's still there."

"Obviously, you couldn't move it."

"I didn't try. I knew in my soul that I wouldn't be able to."

"What else does your soul say, since now you're listening to it?"

"Are you making fun of me, Kamal?"

"Relax, Jerome. All I'm saying is that you seem to know some things instinctively, that's all."

"Yes, I guess I do."

"So, think about it. What else do you know about yourself and the box and all this cross-dimensional crap?"

"I think that when you couldn't see me sitting in the back seat of this cab, I could have probably moved the box."

"Sure, why not," said Kamal sarcastically. "Once in the twilight zone, always in the twilight zone, right?"

"Now you *are* making fun of me."

"No, actually I think you might be right. When Hamm loses consciousness, somehow you shift into the other universe until he comes around again."

"But why, Kamal?"

"How the hell should I know? I just drive a hack. Maybe when the box broke, it attached itself to his consciousness; kind of like an out-of-body experience. You know, astral travel and all that."

"So, if Hamm's body was placed in a coma, even with the use of medicine, he would free me up from this plane and I'd be able to interact in the other one."

"That's right."

"And then I could retrieve the box."

"You got it."

"And maybe I could deliver the box to a location where it could be placed back into a vacuum."

"OK, I'll bite. But for what purpose?"

"Who knows" said Jerome. "But I've always thought that if you can do something, then you should. Just for the sake of accomplishing something."

"You've always thought that, huh?"

"That's right."

"Always, like the whole two weeks your sorry mind has been in existence,"

"I just said always, Kamal, not how long. My life is all about quality, not quantity."

"At least we know you have a sense of humor, Jerome. The way things are going, that will certainly come in handy." They both laughed for a full two blocks. It was a nervous laughter, but a relief just the same.

~

Back in the ICU of Mercy Hospital, Nurse Waters reached up and quickly shut off the alarm triggered by Hamm's monitors. His EEG was no longer admitting alpha brainwaves that are usually present during a sleep state. She knew he was not awake due to the fact that she had just administered a sedative through his IV port a short time earlier. When she entered the unit, she could see that Hamm's eyes were closed, but he was breathing evenly and actually did appear to be sleeping. Only the monitors told her otherwise. She called Hamm's admitting physician and told him of the change. He told her to make sure that one of her staff stays at his bedside at all times. They were to be equipped with a tracheal tube and a 60 cc syringe of epinephrine just in case there were any changes to his autonomic functions.

~

The next time Jerome spoke to Kamal, there was no answer. When Kamal looked to his right and saw just an empty seat, he slammed on the brakes of the taxi. One minute Jerome was sitting there next to him and the next thing, he was gone. "Holy shit," he said. "Jerome, are you still sitting there or what?" He reached his hand over and placed it on the seat. It was still warm. Jerome saw Kamal's hand reach toward him and then pass through his torso and down to the seat below. He reflected on the imaginary therapy sessions in Hamm's office. *Yes, that does indeed feel creepy,* thought Jerome. But it was scary as well. All of a sudden, it dawned on him that were Kamal to pass his hand through his body at the moment of Hamm coming out of his coma . . . he shivered at the thought. He had no desire to become a Siamese twin. Jerome stepped out of the cab without even having to open the door. His feet seemed to find the ground beneath him, but he knew in his heart that it was only an illusion of solid ground. His mind expected to find sure footing beneath him and so he did. He decided to walk up to W 76th Street and Columbus Avenue. If nothing else, he could make a determination as to whether or not he could physically interact with the glass box.

~

The next time Kamal heard Jerome's voice, it was coming from the back seat of his taxi. Jerome had come back to the car and waited in the back seat for the change in Hamm's consciousness. It was less than an hour after he had left the cab and the visibly shaken Kamal.

"I'm back, Kamal," said Jerome.

Kamal again stood on the brakes and said, "Shit Jerome, you scared the hell out of me. I'm not ever going to get used to you winking on an off like a God-damned light for Christ's sake!"

"I'm sorry, Kamal. I don't think there's an easy way to warn you that it's coming. I'm either here or I'm not."

"Where did you go?"

"W 76th Street and Columbus Avenue."

"Somehow I knew you were going to say that. OK, spill it."

"I could feel the box. I could pick up the box. I picked up the box. I took the box."

"Don't say it, Jerome . . ." said Kamal weakly.

"You guessed it. I've got the box."

"In my cab," said Kamal with clear resignation filling his voice.

"I couldn't just leave it there. It could be important."

"So where is it now, exactly?" asked Kamal.

"Right next to me on the back seat."

"Can you see it?"

"Yes."

"Can you still feel it?"

"Nope. My hand passes right through it just like before."

"What the hell did you bring it back to my cab for?"

"Because now we know where it is."

"We knew before. According to you, it was on the sidewalk. You should have left it there."

"Why?" asked Jerome.

"Because moving it was temporary. When this cab moves away, the box will stay where it is. This cab and everything in it is in a different dimension, remember?"

"But now I know it can be moved. Now we can find out how to place it in a vacuum back in the other universe."

"What's that supposed to accomplish?"

"I have no idea. But if nothing else, I might get my memory back. It's worth a try."

"If you turn out to be a rich guy or something, remember, the meter is still running."

"I know."

~

Chapter Eight

Nurse Waters had just retrieved Dr. Hamm from radiology where he had just undergone a cranial cat-scan. His neural surgeon, Dr. Berger, ordered it as a result of his slipping back into a coma for no apparent reason. There was a fair degree of trauma and lacerations to the posterior, cranial-cavity housing the medulla oblongata, and the surgeon applied a temporary suture to stop the bleeding. He knew that radiology might disclose the presence of a foreign body in Hamm's skull, and the cat-scan was likely to reveal it. His worst fears were realized when the radiologist read the film. He called Berger immediately and told him of his findings.

"Dr. Burger," he began.

Burger having recognized his voice and expecting the call answered, "Dr. Patel, I have been looking forward to this call."

"I wish I had good news, Dr. Burger," said Patel.

"Please, call me Helmut, Dr. Patel."

"And you may call me, Dipak, if you will."

"Certainly. I assume you have the results of Dr. Hamm's cranial series?"

"I do."

"You sound like a man with bad news."

"You are very perceptive, Helmut. Naturally, it is your call, but I fear you will be making a visit to his cerebral cortex in the near future."

"You found a mass."

"A small one, yes."

"Small is as big as a dump truck when the proximity to the pituitary is concerned."

"I don't envy your mission in this regard, Helmut."

"And I thank you for your assistance, Dipak. When can I see the plates?"

"They are in your inbox as we speak. There is a link, which will take you to the display. Pay particular attention to the sixth jpeg in the series, Helmut. The shadow in the lower left quadrant is definitely not a biologic entity."

"A foreign mass, then."

"That would be my assertion, but you won't know for sure until it is removed."

"And I have to ask, does is look anything like a benign fatty tumor?"

"The shadow is much darker than a mere capsule, Helmut. If the damned thing was in my head, I'd want it removed."

"I understand. Thank you for your help, Dipak."

"You are most welcome. Enjoy the rest of your day, Helmut."

"And you as well," said Burger breaking the connection. He went to the laptop on an adjacent desk and clicked on the icon for the radiology screens. When he entered Hamm's name, the screen came to life with a series of twenty-two images from the cat-scan. The sixth jpeg showed the mass lodged in anterior cranial cavity. It was shadowed in darkness, although the edges almost appeared to glow with an internal source of light, which he deemed extremely doubtful. Fortunately, there didn't seem to be any apparent swelling of the meninges of the brain or the connective tissue of the spinal cord, but he knew that the immune system was poised to respond to any foreign substance at any time. He contacted nurse Waters and told her to prep Hamm for surgery. The site was to be irrigated with an antibiotic solution, and an ice pack would be applied for five-minute intervals at the top of each hour to retard, if not suppress operative bleeding. Dr. Burger was wishing he were still in bed and all of the incidents of this day only a bad dream. With Hamm dropping in and out of a coma, he couldn't legally sign the necessary forms to release Burger of any liability should anything go wrong during the procedure. But he knew the prominent analyst personally and felt that if the positions were reversed, Hamm would take the same risk for him. When all the malpractice demons and their accompanying, requisite attorneys settled all of the dust of litigation, humanity must be given a fair shot at doing the right thing for the right reason. Although exposing the brain to oxygen always presented a certain degree of danger, the films showed that the area where the mass was located was well away from any major artery that might be compromised. He knew that in most cases, swelling of the meninges was a shortcut to the morgue, and nothing would be more consequential than doing nothing for fear of legal repercussions. He prayed on the way to the surgical scrub-room as was his usual practice.

~

Jerome and Kamal were doing what hacks do best; they were taking fares around Port Authority and delivering them uptown to the usual N.Y.C. destinations. New York City had so much to offer, providing you had deep pockets. A draft beer might cost you eight dollars, but you might be able to enjoy it on the eighty-eighth floor of The Empire State Building. Jerome, as co-pilot, handled luggage and made small talk when the riders demanded it, leaving Kamal to do the driving and combat avoidance of the hectic traffic conditions. When the cab became empty, Kamal said to Jerome, "I still have to eat, Jerome. I might have traveled down the rabbit hole with you, but my job demands that I pick up passengers when I'm not dealing with the Mad Hatter."

"It's not a problem, Kamal. Do you hear me complaining?"

"The night is young."

"What's that supposed to mean?" asked Jerome.

"Where did you sleep last night?"

"Right next to Alice, now that you mentioned the rabbit hole."

"You mean the park?"

"That's right."

"The bronze statue?"

"Right underneath the hedge behind it."

"I have a sofa you can crash on if you want," said Kamal.

"I'm not a charity case."

"The fuck you're not. You have no money, no clean clothes, no memory, and no damned clue as to what you need to do to get your life back in order. I'd call that a charity case."

"I'm fine in the park."

"Fine. Suit yourself, Jerome. Just remember I offered."

"I appreciate it, Kamal. Needless to say, you caught me at a bad time. I'm not even sure what universe I'll be in tomorrow morning."

"Well, if it's this one, I'll meet you at the Carnegie around noon if you want."

"Thank you, Kamal. Yes, I do want. You're a good friend, and you don't even know me."

"I like to think I'm a good judge of character."

"That means a lot to me, Kamal."

"Just prove me right, OK?"

"I'm workin' on it."

"So what about your shrink guy?"

"Dr. Hamm? I'd say he's still conscious for the moment. When he's awake, I have substance in this dimension just like I do now. When I left you earlier, he must have gone down again into a coma."

"It can't be much fun for you blinking on and off like that."

"That's not the worst part."

"What do you mean, Jerome?"

"I think it's killing me, Kamal."

"What are you talking about?"

"Going back and forth between the different branes of existence. I think I'm shoving matter out of the way every time I enter a universe. I'm just lucky I haven't come back in a wall or something. But I know it's messing me up. I haven't had a bowel movement in a pretty long time. Maybe a week or more."

"That's more information than I want, Jerome."

"I'm just saying, I think my intestines are frozen or something. If I don't stabilize pretty soon, I know it's going to kill me."

"So, what's the answer?"

"Hamm has to either get better or go away."

"Go away, huh? Are you contemplating murder, Jerome?"

"No, Kamal. If it comes to that I'll go peacefully. I just might ask you to help me along."

"Forget it, Jerome. I won't have any part in your death."

"I may be dead already. I had visions of therapy with Hamm in his office. I know now they never really happened, but I seem to remember him telling me that I passed over to the other side."

"I hope he's wrong, Jerome. You're starting to scare me. If you're dead, then what does that make me?"

"Don't worry about it, Kamal. You're just a witness."

"Lucky me, huh?"

"Yeah, lucky you."

~

Chapter Nine

The statue in the park that Kamal alluded to was that of Alice in Wonderland from the story by Robert Louis Stevenson. It was actually called, Alice Trough the Looking Glass and with regard to the recent past of Jerome Cleveland, a most appropriate place to place his head for the warm August evening. As it was a popular place in the park, Jerome found that he was not alone. There was a gathering of street performers who often congregated there to compare the present *pulse* of the city. New York City is a living, breathing place, which is rarely static in nature. It is forever changing with the attitudes of the tourists regarding relative safety from crime or terrorism, the weight of the dollar against the yen and a thousand other aspects of negotiating the most powerful city in the world. After 911, Mayor Giuliani placed 18% more patrolmen on the street and transformed the image of the city to one of safety and security in the face of those who would design to do her harm. It was an *"in your face"* dare to be oblivious of the threat to national security with the understanding that, *"If they make us change our way of living, they win."* Nobody beats New York City. You can wound her and threaten her again with violence, and she will stand tall and fearless once again. Her greatest asset is the people. Both the residents and the visitors alike. All people work together to make the city great. You can leave your heart in San Francisco, but your brain will probably always remain in New York, New York.

The statue of Alice in the park is made completely of bronze. Its thousands of pounds of metal were all cast and hammered together in nineteen fifty-nine building a solid statue of a little girl. Unlike most sculptures, children are invited to climb, touch and crawl all over little Alice and her friends. In fact, through the decades thousands of hands and feet have literally polished parts of the statue's surface smooth. Alice is sitting on a giant mushroom reaching toward a pocket watch held by the White Rabbit. Peering over her shoulder is the Cheshire Cat, surrounded by the Dormouse, Alice's cat Dinah, and the Mad Hatter all fused together in a mass of Lewis Carroll memorabilia.

Jerome was looking over the statue when a juggler came up to him and tapped him on the shoulder. He was dressed in a dark flowered, long sleeve shirt and a brown suede vest over his distressed, designer Levis. He had long blond hair pulled back in a ponytail and a small canine companion at his side. The Juggler said, "That's a major good gag, man."

"What?" asked Jerome.

"The vanishing thing you do. I watched you over on Seventh Ave. Man that was cool. David Blane's got nothing on you. Copperfield either."

"I'm not sure what you're talking about," said Jerome.

"Sure. I get it. You don't want to give it away. Well, I'm not your competition, man. I just juggle. I was just giving credit where credit is due. You are the bomb."

"I'm not any bomb, sir. I'm just a tired traveler who would enjoy a little rest under the hedges here."

"Lay it down, man. I won't bother you."

"Thank you," said Jerome although he wasn't sure whether or not he could close his eyes in this circumstance. Now that he has unintentionally drawn attention to himself, he had to approach his circumstances a bit differently. He wondered if he could ever master the art of sleeping with one eye open.

~

When Dr. Burger reached the operating theater, the anesthesiologist was just briefing his patient, Dr. Jerry Hamm, about the forthcoming procedure. Hamm said to him, "I'm finally going to get some sleep."

"Oh, you betcha'," said *The Sandman*, a euphemism given to him by his O.R. colleagues.

Burger walked up to the table and took Hamm by the hand, "Are you ready for this, Jerry?"

"More than ready, Helmut," said Hamm. "I feel like I'm stuck in a revolving door."

"We should be done in about an hour," said Burger. "Then you should be stabilized to the point where we can admit you to a room."

"Wonderful," said Hamm dryly.

"I'll bring you some real food, my friend," said Burger.

"I will definitely owe you one, Helmut." Hamm chuckled, which Burger took to be a good sign. A lot of a patient's recovery was dependent on attitude as much as procedure. Burger knew that his good friend Jerry had a good mental outlook and a lust for life despite his recent breakup with his wife of seventeen years. Their separation was amicable and neither party held any ill will toward their ex-spouse. They merely mutually agreed that they had found each other too early in life having begun in high school. They would always remain good friends.

"Let's open up this can and see what we've got," said Burger jovially.

"If you find any beans in there, leave em' where they are, Helmut."

"It's a deal," he said with a nod to The Sandman. A valve was opened in Hamm's IV and The Sandman said, "You know the drill, Dr. Hamm. Start at one hundred and count backwards."

Jerry Hamm only got to ninety-one before he was under the anesthesia.

~

Jerome was awakened by snoring. He looked to his right and saw the sleeping form of a blond woman next to him. Her face was very round, and her hair was spiked in a way that made him think of the Statue of Liberty. He noticed some very large diamond studded earrings and a matching diamond set as a pendant in a gold chain around her neck. He was a bit surprised to see she was topless, and her shirt was rolled up into a pillow beneath her head. He decided not to bother her and went back to sleep. The next morning, he got up and found the woman sitting Indian style nearby sipping coffee out of a large Starbucks container. When she saw that he was awake, she reached out to a small, white bag in front of her and retrieved another container of coffee. She rose to her feet and brought it over to Jerome who was just wiping the sleep from his eyes. "There's cream in the bag, but I pegged you for a black coffee guy. Am I right?"

"Yes, thank you. Black coffee would be very nice."

She handed him the container, "I'm Cookie," she said smiling.

"Jerome," was all he said shaking the cobwebs out of his mind. It had been a rough week so far.

"Art says you're a magic man."

"Who is Art?" asked Jerome sleepily.

"Art the gypsy. He juggles over on Seventh Avenue near the 59th Street entrance. You know, right near the coaches with those tired looking horses."

"I'm not sure I know him," said Jerome.

"Well, he sure knows you. He says you're the real thing. He says we'll probably see you on The Tonight Show soon with Jimmy Fallon."

"I don't know Jimmy Fallon either," said Jerome.

"Of course, you don't, silly," she said screwing up her eyes and giggling. "He's famous."

"Supposedly, I'm kind of famous, too."

"Oh really?" asked Cookie. "What's your last name, Jerome?"

"It's Cleveland."

"Jerome Cleveland," repeated Cookie. "No, I don't think you're famous. At least I never heard of you."

"That makes two of us."

"What are you talking about?" she asked.

"I've never heard of me either. I know my name, but that's about all."

"Art says you know magic. He says you're the bomb."

"I don't know any magic, Cookie."

"I know, you're saving it for the marks. I don't blame you, Jerome. I just want you to remember me when you're rich and famous, OK?"

"You'll have to get in line, Cookie. I'm hearing that a lot lately."

"Did you really lose your memory, Jerome?"

"I'm afraid so," he said in an exasperated exhalation.

"That's so cool," said Cookie giggling.

"No, it's not."

"Well, there's a lot of crap about my life I'd like to forget."

"Oh?" asked Jerome wiping sleep from his eyes with a yawn.

"My name, for one thing."

"What's wrong with Cookie?"

"That's not my real name."

"What is your real name?" asked Jerome.

"You wouldn't believe me if I told you."

"Try me."

"OK, it's Jane."

"What's the matter with Jane?"

"My last name is Doe."

"So, you're Jane Doe. What about it?"

"You really have lost your memory."

"Why do you say that, Cookie?"

"My parents grew up in the fifties. They thought it would be a hoot to name me Jane Doe."

"So, now you're Cookie Doe."

"That's right. Do you like it?"

"I suppose," said Jerome.

"You don't recognize me, do you?"

"No, Cookie. Should I?"

"I'm the girl on the syrup bottle."

"That's nice."

"No, really. Aunt Jenny's Pure Maple Syrup. My parents were Aunt Jenny. At least they started the company."

"I'm not familiar with it," said Jerome.

"It's the biggest name in maple syrup in probably the whole world. And it's all mine."

"You own the company?" asked Jerome.

"Yupper," said Cookie.

"And you sleep in the park."

"When the weather's like this, yeah."

"Where do you live?"

"I have the penthouse at Sixty-fifth and Park."

"You live there alone?"

"Yeah, I'm an orphan."

"Oh, I'm sorry," said Jerome.

"Don't be. My parents lived a long and happy life. They died in their late eighties."

"How old are you, Cookie?" asked Jerome.

"I'm twenty-seven. They had me in their sixties, but they were great parents."

"And you live in a penthouse on Park Avenue all by yourself?"

"So far, but some of the street performers crash there sometimes."

"That's nice," he said wondering if this young woman was putting him on.

"Are you hungry?"

"Not really," said Jerome. "I should be, but I think my stomach is messed up."

"That's too bad. Well, I'm hungry. I'm going to go to Rumplemayer's for some eggs Benedict. You can come with me if you want. Breakfast is on me."

"I think I'll pass, Cookie," said Jerome. It was then he noticed that she was barefoot. "Do they let you in without shoes?" he asked her.

"I know the hostess and she keeps a pair of sandals for me at the base of her lectern. I've also got a pair stashed at The Tavern on the Green."

"Why no shoes?" he asked.

"I like the feeling of the grass under my feet and I don't want to carry them."

"Oh," was all Jerome could say.

"OK, well it was nice to meet you, Jerome. Thanks for sleeping with me. I know we didn't do anything, but I never like to sleep alone."

"Don't mention it," said Jerome.

"Are you going to sleep here again tonight?" she asked him.

"Probably."

"Well, maybe I'll see you later."

"Maybe so."

Cookie leaned over and gave Jerome a kiss on the cheek, "Hope so," she said gliding away. She moved like a dancer, and

Jerome found himself wondering if she had some talent that she displayed as one of the street performers like Art the gypsy. Her story, about owning some gigantic syrup company didn't ring true, but then again, his story were no more unbelievable if he were to offer it to her. Kamal had a hard time swallowing it, and he had actually witnessed his disappearances first-hand. Giving him a cup of coffee was a nice gesture on Cookie's part. He hoped he could somehow return the favor when he got his life straightened out. He finished the container and tossed it into a nearby trash can. He had to kill some time because Kamal said he would see him around lunch time at the Carnegie. He decided that the library would be a good place to do some research. They probably offered computer terminals for free, but he hoped he wouldn't need a card to use one.

~

Chapter Ten

The procedure on Hamm was text book. It took less than an hour as predicted by Burger and a foreign object was removed and proved to be a small piece of glass. Despite the successful operation by Burger, The Sandman was unable to bring Hamm back up from the anesthesia. He had no clue or explanation for the difficulty he was having. Hamm's vital signs were strong, and he never really took him down as low as an induced coma state, but he seemed to remain there anyway. He said to Burger, "I can't figure out what's keeping him under, Helmut. He should have come right up easily, just like clockwork."

"It's got to be his history," said Burger. "He's been in and out of a coma so often that his autonomics are probably hyper-mobile. It's become too easy for his mind to just rest there."

"It's your call, Helmut," said The Sandman. "I can introduce a stimulant, but I don't recommend it for now."

"I think he's out of the woods now. I'm going to admit him and just wait it out and monitor him. Put the order in to remove his IV port. We can always poke him again if we need to. When he wakes up, I want the transition to be as stress-free as possible. His mind will do the healing from now on."

"You got it," said The Sandman writing down the order for the nurses.

~

When Jerome got to the New York Public Library, it didn't take him very long to determine that Dr. Hamm was once again in a coma. He was once again invisible to the people around him and the materials within the library were useless to him. He knew that without substance in this plane or brane of strings, he could not manipulate one of the computer terminals even if he were allowed to use it. He had no choice but to return to Mercy Hospital and try to gain access once again to Dr. Hamm's bedside. He found the task to be a lot easier this time around. When he returned to the ICU, it was only a short while until he overheard one of the nurses mentioning the room where Dr. Hamm was placed. Unfortunately, he was accompanied by a respiratory therapist who was sitting in a chair reading a book. He knew when Dr. Hamm came out of the coma, he would suddenly appear out of thin air and totally freak out the therapist. He had no choice but to wait it out until there was a shift change or she had to use the restroom. After twenty nervous minutes, he suddenly got his chance. Sure enough, nature called, and the therapist entered the restroom in Dr. Hamm's room and closed the door. Jerome went to his bedside and reached down to take his hand. Dr. Hamm's eyes once again opened, and he smiled up at Jerome standing beside him. Jerome, it would seem, was suddenly hit by a sledge-hammer of lucidity. His entire collection of memories came flooding back into his mind, and the incidents of the past two weeks were unfolded before him and placed in their proper perspective at last. The mysteries of how the recent events came to pass were fully disclosed, and his considerable intellect was restored in all its glory. He knew who Jerome Cleveland was. He knew about the procedure he had invented to place an isolated, sub-atomic particle in a vacuum tube and accelerate the tube itself within the hadron collider rather than only the particle itself. The acceleration was stored as a kinetic energy event rather than only static potential energy. He remembered the consortium at the planetarium within The Museum of Natural History on 82nd Street and Central Park West. He remembered asking his therapist, Jerry Hamm to accompany him there where he was to receive an award from the International Board of Theoretical Physics. It was understood that a Nobel Prize was soon to follow.

Tears began to well up in Jerome's eyes as he looked down to Dr. Hamm lying on the hospital bed before him and he said, "Jerry, I'm back."

"Entirely?" asked Hamm.

"I've got the whole picture now. All of the pictures. It's like I've never been away, although I also have memories of the last two weeks during my amnesia."

"That's wonderful, Jerome. I suppose I have you to thank for waking me out of the coma once again," he said.

"Probably," said Jerome. "I think when the vacuum tube fractured, the particles were passed right through my head as isolated neutrinos and lodged in your visual cortex just above your spinal cord. That's why you could see me on the alternate brane of strings when nobody else could manage it. Then when I learned that we never actually had our therapy sessions during the last two weeks, it all became clear that our entities were joined together and only existed deeply embedded in your mind. They had to be separated by removing the piece of glass from your brain. I feel certain that I have

71

a handle on that other universe that has been haunting me from the other side."

"So, the other side is not really death. Is that what you're saying, Jerome?"

"I'm not saying I understand it, Jerry. All I know is that I think I need to table my research for a while. I'm confident I'll get it all worked out in time."

"Perhaps you're right," said Hamm. "What are your plans?"

"I think I'm going to become a street performer for a little while."

"Oh? What is your talent, Jerome?"

"Watch this," he said with a smile. His image began to fade like a gossamer shroud until at last there was no one standing in the room at all. Hamm was alone and yet he couldn't help asking, "Are you still here, Jerome?"

The door to Jerry Hamm's room then opened and closed again. A smile came to his lips, and he closed his eyes once again to sleep.

~

Kamal's taxi was double parked on Seventh Avenue near the Carnegie when Jerome sauntered up to the driver's door a new man. He was once again a complete man with all his faculties intact and the realization that he was the first to bridge the vast chasm between two of the eleven string dimensions. He chose to denote the number nine to the brane of strings he had traveled back and forth from. In the back of his mind, he supposed that word play was at the heart of that particular label. D-9 sounded an awful lot like denial, which is what he was feeling regarding his acceptance of the situation. He decided to just flow with it and perhaps use his new-found talent for dimension travel sparingly. He was obviously only joking with Dr. Hamm when suggested he would act as a street performer. But he wasn't ready to walk away from his interest in Cookie Doe. He broached the subject as soon as he slid in beside Kamal, who was munching on his pastrami sandwich, "Kamal, I met a girl."

"Yippee," he said with his mouth full. "Does that mean she's buying you lunch these days instead of me?" he asked between chews.

"I told you I'd pay you back, Kamal. Today is the day."

"Don't tell me," said Kamal as he stopped chewing and stared at Jerome knowing what was coming.

"I know it all. I've got the world by the balls, Kamal, and you were here to witness it first hand."

"Just what am I witnessing?" asked Kamal almost afraid of what was about to be revealed.

"I know who Jerome Cleveland is, Kamal. Soon the whole world will know as well. I am the first man to travel between dimensions at will."

"At will? You mean you can do it all by yourself?"

"Anytime I want."

"Now you are going to rob a bank, right?" he asked jokingly.

"I don't have to, Kamal. I've got all the money I could ever want."

"What? You're rich?" asked Kamal.

"You betcha'," said Jerome. "I've got an account that is tied to a Swiss bank through an institution called *Partners of Geneva*. All of us physicists who travel abroad to the hadron collider have a similar account."

"Does that mean I'm gonna' get my eighteen bucks back?" he asked going back to his sandwich.

"Let me ask you, Kamal; do you own this cab?"

"I drive this cab, Jerome. United City Transit is the company that owns it."

"Would you like your own cab, Kamal?"

"What are you kidding? I've wanted to become an indie for about twelve years now; ever since I moved here from upstate New York."

"Well, let's go shopping."

"You really mean it, don't you, Jerome?"

"I surely do. Let's go buy you a cab, and then, I'd like you to meet a nice kid I met in the park."

"What's her name?" asked Kamal.

"Cookie," said Jerome.

"Oh, the syrup lady," said Kamal smiling. He started to chuckle at the stunned expression on Jerome's face.

"I guess I shouldn't be surprised, should I, Kamal? This has been one hell of a week."

"You got that right," said Kamal.

~

Chapter Eleven

Kamal and Jerome spotted Art the gypsy juggling in front of The Shops at Columbus Circle on 58th Street. Art and his Jack Russell terrier, Roadie, *whom he always referred to as his Jack Russell Terrorist,* had attracted a rather large crowd in front of Equinox Fitness Club. Roadie was sporting a little Roadie-sized fedora on his head, and had a small basket around his neck attached to his collar for the purpose of collecting Art's tips. Jerome asked Kamal, "Pull over for a minute, and give me a fifty, will ya'?"

"A fifty? What? Are you going to juice Roadie's basket or something?"

"If you mean am I going to give Art a tip, then yes."

Jerome took the fifty and hopped out of the cab. He walked up to Roadie and placed the bill in the basket making sure that Art noticed the denomination. Art nodded his thanks and never missed a beat with his juggling pins as he said, "Nice to see you, Mr. Bomb, for the time being that is."

Jerome chuckled and said to him, "I'm giving up the act. You've seen the last performance."

"Too bad," said Art. "You would have gone viral, my friend."

"Take it easy," said Jerome.

"Arrrf!" said Rodie.

"You said it," said Art to his canine sidekick.

When Jerome got back in the cab, he said to Kamal, "Where to now?"

"Jersey," said Kamal. "I know a Lexus dealer in Fort Lee who can give me a good deal."

"Lexus?" asked Jerome. "Who said anything about a Lexus?"

"How much money do you have in that Partners of Geneva account, Jerome?"

"A Lexus it is," said Jerome. He reflected that the answer to Kamal's question was upwards of twenty-million Swiss francs.

"How did you know the name of Art's dog?" asked Jerome.

"Simple. I know Art. I know most of the street performers and sometimes I hang with them at Cookie's crib."

"Does she really own the whole floor of that condo?"

"She could own the whole building if she wanted to. By the way, she offered me my own cab as well, but I couldn't take her up on it."

"Why not?"

"I don't like strings, man. I like to stay foot-loose and fancy free."

"But you don't mind taking a gift from me," Jerome said dully. "A Lexus, no less."

"That's different. That's payback."

"For two sandwiches and a few rides around town?"

"Call it interest on the loan. And have you seen the price of gas lately?"

"Oh, naturally. The price of gas," said Jerome facetiously. "But, honestly, Kamal, it won't even make a hiccup in my account. You could have asked for a Lamborghini."

"No room for passengers," said Kamal. "Besides, those things are a speeding ticket waiting to happen."

"So, what about your home? Do you own it?"

"Not hardly. I rent a place over in Hoboken, New Jersey."

"Would you like to live in the city?"

"I can't afford it."

"I might be able to make you a sweet deal, Kamal. I plan to buy a condo here near the park. You could rent from me."

"Thanks just the same, Jerome, but I don't think I could handle a roommate. Remember, footloose, fancy free?"

"I got you, Kamal. It was just a suggestion. Maybe I can buy a duplex in a brownstone up in Harlem."

"Now you're talkin'," said Kamal. "I love the brownstones up there."

~

After Kamal and Jerome had purchased the Lexus from the dealer in Fort Lee, New Jersey, they both drove back to the city in a two-car convoy. Kamal led the way in his old cab with the broken right tail light, and Jerome followed in the Lexus. They made their way across the Hudson River by way of the Lincoln Tunnel and turned downtown to the parking lot of U.C.T., or United City Transit Inc. Jerome was sad to leave the company as he had made some good friends there in the past twelve years. There were only well wishes for him on the part of his fellow employees and he promised to make regular trips back to the lot to keep in touch. Even Kamal's supervisor wished him well and knew there would soon be someone to take his place on the team of city hacks. Kamal knew it would take a few days to gain an independent, gypsy cab license and apply for his own insurance. In the mean time he assured Jerome, "I'm all yours, man. You've got yourself your own personal driver for the next few days. I can't work without a license and insurance. I've still got my driver's license, but I had to surrender my chauffer's license when I left U.C.T."

"Take me to Cookie's crib, Kamal. I wan't to thank her for the cup of coffee she gave me."

"Oh yeah, what are you gonna' buy her, a Lear Jet?"

"She doesn't need anything, Kamal, except perhaps a friend."

"Gotcha'."

~

When they got to Cookie's condominium at Six-Fifty Park Avenue, Cookie was not in. Freddie, the doorman knew Kamal and welcomed them both to enter the lobby and speak with Alphonse, the concierge, who rang up Cookie's butler, Watson. When Kamal heard Watson's voice on the intercom, he said, "I'm here with a friend of Cookie's, Watson. Would it be alright if we come on up and wait for her here?"

"You're welcome anytime, Kamal, as you well know," said Watson.

"Thanks, Watson."

"I'll join you for cocktails in the library, Kamal," said Watson.

"I'll tell Cookie you're drinking on duty again, Watson."

"Very good, Sir. I'm sure she'll issue me my walking papers directly."

"I'm sure she could find someone a lot better to run her household," said Kamal with false severity.

"Screw you very much, Sir," said Watson with a chuckle. Jerome soon understood that Kamal and Watson were very good friends.

The inside of the condominium at Six-Fifty Park Avenue took Jerome's breath away. In the two-story foyer, there was a prominentely featured twenty-foot, hanging glass work of art by Dale Chihuly. Its aquatic theme featured a huge manta-ray that was wrapped by a medley of dolphin, sharks and moray eels. The floor was covered nearly wall to wall with a twenty by thirty-foot custom made, Surya Adana, hand knotted, New Zealand wool rug. The six armchairs placed against the wall were Chippendale and the, nine-foot tall, double entrance doors to the ballroom beyond were solid, hand-carved ebony frescos of the Garden of Eden.

"Nice digs," said Jerome to Watson.

"We like to think so," said Watson.

"Are you the butler?" he asked.

"Yes, Sir, and I cook as well," said Watson.

"Watson is a graduate of the Culinary Institute of America," said Kamal.

"Don't get me started, Kamal. My stomach is growling already," said Jerome.

"I could whip you up a spinach, mushroom and truffle quiche in about twenty minutes," said Watson.

"You know that's not really my style, Watson," said Kamal.

"I wasn't talking to you, Mr. Cheeseburger in Paradise," said Watson with false contempt.

"Just the whiskey, Watson," said Jerome. "I'm sure that Cookie has a good one on hand."

"Several, actually. Do you prefer single malt?"

"Dewer's would be fine."

"As you wish, Sir."

"You can call me Jerome, Watson. And do you have a first name?"

"It's Woodhouse, Jerome. I still haven't forgiven my parents."

"I'll call you Watson."

"Very good, Jerome," said Watson chuckling.

When Watson was pouring drinks from the cart caddie, Jerome asked him, "Just how big *is* this place?"

"It's something over twelve thousand square feet I'm led to believe."

"I believe it," said Jerome. "A lot of house for just one woman, wouldn't you say?"

"Well, she might want to put in a basketball court. You never know," said Watson smiling.

~

Chapter Twelve

Cookie found them in the Library a short time later. She winked at Kamal and reached out to briefly grasp his hand as she passed. Then she came up to Jerome and wrapped her arms around him. "What a nice surprise, Jerome. How did you find your way here?" she asked knowingly looking at Kamal.

"Guilty as charged," said Kamal. "He said he was a friend of yours."

"And so he is," said Cookie. "We shared a patch of grass in the park."

"I wish you wouldn't sleep there, Cookie," said Kamal. "You have a lawn of your own on the roof here."

It's not the same, Kamal. In the park, there're birds and rabbits and a lot of my friends sleep there as well. You know they look out for me."

"I know, Cookie. But I also know that some weirdoes hang out there as well. I swear you have a guardian angel."

"I have several, Kamal, so stop worrying."

"I hope you don't mind us helping ourselves to your scotch, Cookie," said Jerome.

"Not at all. You know I have some Glencarrie, don't you."

"Too fancy for my taste, Cookie. I prefer a blend."

"Actually, I don't really even like the stuff. Watson usually just makes me a seabreeze."

81

"All this money wasted on a troglodyte," said Watson stiffly.

"Shuuud up, Watson. I can't help it if it tastes like kerosene."

"Kerosene doesn't cost two-hundred dollars a gallon, Madam."

"Make me a sea breeze please."

"As you wish," said Watson with a slight bow.

"So, Jerome, have any luck getting back the story of your life?"

"That's an interesting way to put it, but yes, I have. I remember everything now."

"And?"

"I'm not sure you want to know, Cookie."

"You kill anybody?"

"Not that I know of," said Jerome.

"Well, that's good enough for me."

"That's it? That's all you need to know about me?"

"I trust Kamal. I figure you'll tell me about yourself when you're ready."

"You are a remarkable woman, Cookie."

"Not so remarkable. I just think I'm a good judge of character. Take Watson for instance; he's probably the best butler in all of New York."

"Fuck you, Madam," with mock seriousness.

"See? You see how polite he is? And he sometimes leaves the room *before* he farts."

"I won't the next time, I assure you," said Watson earnestly.

They all got a good laugh at the banter between the lady of the house and her faithful servant.

When she wiped the tears of laughter from her eyes, she asked Watson, "What are you cooking tonight?"

"I wasn't aware I was cooking, Madam. I offered Mister Jerome one of my famous quiches, but he decided to pass."

"Call it a rain check, Watson," said Jerome.

"He only passed because he's never tasted your cooking. Why don't we show him one of your specialties tonight?"

"As you wish, Madam. Perhaps a standing rib roast with Yorkshire Pudding and garlic mashed potatoes."

"Sounds yummy, and what else?"

"Asparagus spears seared in sesame oil and almond slivers, and for dessert, a homemade, Granny Smith apple pie a la mode."

"This is definitely my favorite dimension," Jerome said to Kamal as an aside.

"What?" asked Cookie.

"It's a long story," said Kamal, "but a good one, Cookie. You're gonna' love it."

~

Watson's dinner was a huge success. The succulent, rare to medium-rare rib roast was served with a creamy horseradish sauce and a very dry cabernet from Napa Valley California. The potatoes and asparagus were done to perfection, and when it came time for dessert, all were in agreement that they needed to rest for a while away from the table. After some cordials in the library, they decided to put off Watson's apple pie and walk off their dinner with an early evening, quarter mile trek to the park. There was a rising, gibbous moon on the eastern horizon just peeking over the buildings of upper

Manhattan. The horse drawn carriages were clip-clopping down the paved streets through the park, and a dozen dog owners had been chastised by their canine friends for neglecting them during the day and were coerced into multiple tosses of the Frisbee. Lovers were lying wrapped around each other on blankets strewn across Sheep Meadow, and Cookie and her three escorts were contemplating the ramifications of their friend Jerome's new-found ability to transport himself between dimensions. Cookie and Watson thought they were just going along with the gag, but Kamal knew from personal experience that Jerome was not joking about his extraordinary ability. None of them besides Jerome knew the ins and outs of particle physics so they just had to take his word for it and bare with his braggadocio until Cookie finally asked him, "OK Jerome, let's see it. Put your money where your mouth is."

Jerome looked at Cookie and decided to take a calculated risk. He abruptly took her in his arms and said, "I'll do you one better, Cookie." The air shimmered around them with a silver aura and they seemed to pulsate for a moment before suddenly winking out altogether in the blink of an eye. They were gone. There seemed to be no sign that they were ever there in the first place. Kamal was not as taken aback at Watson who said, "What the bloody hell?"

"You thought he was just shitting you didn't you, Watson?"

"Well, I knew he had some kind of revelation regarding his work, but nothing like this. Where did they go?"

"Nowhere, actually. And everywhere, depending how you look at it. They are still right here and can probably still see and hear us."

"Why, that's preposterous," said Watson.

"You saw it with your own eyes."

"I don't know what I saw. Perhaps multiple hypnosis. He's put us under some kind of spell."

"No, Watson. He's the real deal. I've seen it all before, but he never had control until now."

"What do you mean control?"

"Before, he was not in charge of when the transfer took place. His psychiatrist, Dr. Hamm, was in a coma over at Mercy Hospital. When he came out of the coma, Jerome came back to this dimension."

"I think this is all some kind of ruse, Kamal. Why would you do this to us?"

"It's no ruse, Watson. Jerome is the first one in history to do it. He can travel between dimensions, and now, apparently, he can take others with him as well. I had no idea about that until it happened. Plus, I have a sneaking suspicion that he didn't either."

"That's quite a risk to take if what you're saying is true."

"I agree," said Kamal.

Cookie and Jerome were witnessing the conversation between Watson and Kamal, and when she fully understood the situation and the risk that Jerome was taking with her, she was livid. She slapped him hard on the cheek. "You bastard!"

"Calm down, Cookie."

"Calm down? What gives you the right to drag me along into your nightmare, Jerome? Just where the fuck are we?"

"We're still here in the park. We're just on a different set of dimensional strings. I call it D-9."

"I call it insane," she said hotly. "What if we can't get back?"

"Relax, Cookie. Just hold onto me tightly and we'll go right back."

"I don't think I want to go anywhere near you, Jerome."

"You have to, Cookie. I can't get you back unless you are in contact with me, get it?"

"No, I don't." She started to cry. "What else is in this . . . dimension of yours? Are there monsters here?"

"I don't think so," said Jerome. "I think that this dimension is just like ours except the people here can't experience us. The good thing is, we can still experience the other dimension from this one. It's like we can eves drop on the whole world if we want to."

"Well, I don't want to. I want to go back, now, Jerome."

"OK, hold onto me very tightly just to make sure. I'll take us back right away."

Cookie fell into his arms and held on tight. The shimmering aura of silver light pulsated once again and then they passed from D-9 into their original dimension in an instant. Watson and Kamal were looking in another direction and didn't witness the transfer. But Art the gypsy juggler and his sidekick Roadie most certainly did. Art started clapping his hands and proclaimed, "Outstanding, man. That's the most incredible gag I've ever seen in my whole life."

Cookie was still crying and said to Art, "It's not a gag, Art. It's a dangerous fucking game, and I'm not playing anymore." She ran full speed across Sheep Meadow and never looked back. Kamal realizing what had happened turned around and said to him, "Well, that went well."

"She's just frightened, Kamal. She'll come around once she realizes that she is fine physically and was never really at risk."

"Never at risk, huh?"

"No, I don't think so," said Jerome.

"*Think* is the operative word in that sentence, Jerome. You don't know. You're not sure one-hundred percent what you're doing and you're playing with other people's lives."

"Calm down, Kamal," said Jerome.

"Calm down? Let me ask you something; when you are over in the other dimension . . ."

"I call it D-9," said Jerome.

"Whatever. When you are over in D-9, do you have all your smarts?"

"What do you mean?"

"Your intellect. A while back, when you were in that other dimension, you couldn't remember everything. Is it the same way now?"

"Not exactly."

"What does that mean?" asked Jerome.

"All I have to know is how to get back. I don't have to do any computations there, Kamal."

"You don't know that, Jerome. You're playing with fire. And Cookie is a friend of mine. From now on, she's off limits. No more inter-dimensional travel with other people until you know exactly what you're doing."

"I'd like to take a turn," said Watson meekly. "That is, if you don't mind. I'd love to see what another dimension looks like, Jerome."

"Maybe some other time, Watson. I'm going to go after Cookie right now. I've been careless and I need to apologize."

"Yes, you sure do," said Kamal.

~

Chapter Thirteen

Dr. Jerry Hamm had just finished breakfast. It was eggs Benedict that Dr. Burger had brought in from Rumplemayer's on the bottom floor of the St. Moritz Hotel on 59th Street. He also had an apple muffin with a cinnamon sugar glaze that he wrapped in a napkin and was saving for a mid-morning snack. His drink was a one-two punch of cappuccino and Pete's, Columbian coffee with the hopes of kick-starting his day. He was to be released at noon. Dr. Burger chose to look in on him as the first of his rounds for the morning. "I trust you enjoyed your breakfast, Jerry," said Burger.

"I owe you a big one, Helmut."

"I couldn't let you eat that crap they give the other patients."

"And I appreciate it no end, my friend," said Hamm.

"Are you ready to break out of this joint?"

"More than ready, Helmut."

"Have you made arrangements for a ride home?"

"Not yet."

"Your friend Dr. Cleveland has been calling daily for updates of your recovery. Is he a close friend, Jerry?"

"He's more of an acquaintance, Helmut. Actually, he is a former patient."

"Oh?"

"He was in the taxi with me when the accident happened."

"You mean, he's the one?"

"What one is that, Helmut?"

"The one they made all that fuss about. Wasn't he missing for a while?"

"Yes, about a week. He had temporary amnesia. He tells me that he has decided to take up residence here in the city. We're not sure whether or not we will resume therapy."

"Do you trust him?"

"Yes, Helmut. He is an honest man."

"Then perhaps you should let him give you a ride to your home."

"Yes, Helmut. Perhaps I should. Please make arrangements to lift the block on my phone. The next time he calls, I'd like to talk to him."

"As you wish, Jerry. Do I have to say it?"

"Say what, Helmut?"

"You need to rest. No more work for at least a week. Please, plenty of bed rest and take on some help for the next few days."

"I will, my friend. But thank you for worrying about me."

"Think nothing of if, Jerry. Just remember, your job now is recovery. The rest can wait."

~

"Dr. Hamm, I've made a terrible mistake."

"Jerome?"

"I blew it."

"Jerome, is that you?"

"Yes, it's me. Can't you recognize my voice?"

"Slow down, Jerome, what did you blow?"

"I met a girl."

"That sounds very nice."

"No, you don't understand. I don't think she ever wants to see me again, and I can't stop thinking about her. Can I meet you in your office?"

"No, Jerome. I'm closed for business. But you can give me a ride home."

"OK, but when will we be able to talk, about my problem?"

"Which problem is that, Jerome. I think you have a number of them."

"I want some advice about the girl."

"I'm not sure I can help you, Jerome. Matters of the heart are a complicated lot. As you probably know, I am divorced from my wife."

"I don't care anything about that, Dr. Hamm. I'm feeling really unsettled here."

"Well, perhaps you should start by having a little empathy, Jerome. The world does not start and end with your problems. Don't you suppose that I am also unsettled being estranged from my wife of seventeen years?"

"Yes, I know. I'm sorry, Dr. Hamm. It's just that I'm feeling really incomplete right now, and I don't think that I can sleep."

"So then don't."

"What?"

"Don't sleep, Jerome. Stay up all night sleeping under the Alice in Wonderland Statue and ponder the reason you are in the fix you are in right now."

"I have an apartment. Actually, it's a duplex."

"How nice for you."

"What do you mean don't sleep? What kind of advice is that?"

"The only kind I can offer right now. I told you, I'm not seeing patients at the moment."

"But if I pick you up at the hospital, you can talk to me on the ride to your house, right?"

"Yes, Jerome, but I can't be responsible for anything you might take from our conversation. I am in the process of convalescing. I have a great deal of healing to do, and my doctor has made me promise to rest and not resume my practice for at least a week."

"Oh, alright. When are they going to let you go?"

"They said noon. But I know from personal experience that it could be as late as three or four before they dot all the i's and cross all the t's."

"What?"

"Just give me your cell phone number and I'll call you when they are wheeling me down."

"What? Can't you walk?"

"It's just procedure, Jerome. It has something to do with insurance and liability. Everyone gets wheeled down when they are released."

"OK. My number is 212 – 555 – 7069. I'll wait for your call."

"Sounds like a plan. Don't worry about the girl, Jerome. If you can't patch up the tear in your relationship, then it just wasn't meant to be. I've come to accept that eventuality with my own situation. My wife and I will never get back together, but that may well be for the best."

"I'm not going to give up on her, Dr. Hamm."

"We'll talk about it later, Jerome." Hamm broke the connection and started gathering up his clothing from the closet in the corner of his room.

~

Cookie was sitting on a large rock in the middle of Sheep Meadow. Something was licking her ankle. She looked down and wiped the tears from her eyes, "Roadie," she said, "are you trying to tell me that I taste delicious?"

Roadie jumped up onto the rock next to her and began to lick her face. It was amazing how fast the little dog could transform her misery into joy. She loved Roadie and took him into her arms. "You're my boyfriend, aren't you, Roadie? We don't need anyone else to be happy, do we? Why don't we take my jet down to Ecuador and mess with some blue-footed boobies?"

"Arrf!" said Roadie.

"Or maybe some Galapagos tortoises. You could ride on their back and I'll take your picture. That would be one hell of a you-tube picture, wouldn't it? But we'd probably get a fine or something," she said laughing. Laughter was much preferred from what she was feeling a short while ago. She was attracted to Jerome, but she had a number of conflicts running through her mind. The most important one was his flippant attitude regarding her safety. Yes, she took chances. Yes, she had relationships with some of the less desirable members of the city residents, but she was always in control. She was always able to step back and call the shots, until she met Jerome. When he took her into the dimension that he dubbed D-9, she was helpless to do anything about it. None of the people who looked out for her interests and safety could intervene as well. It all happened so fast that she was instantly reduced to someone without power. And for a person who grew up with power, that was unsettling in the least. No one could control Cookie. Not even her parents. No amount of new clothes or new cars could sway her from her expression as one of the fortunate, free-thinking elite, let loose into the New York City young society. And here she was reduced to tears with a Jack Russell Terrorist licking her face to make it all better.

~

The next time a phone call was placed to Jerry Hamm's hospital room, it rang on the phone at his bedside. All calls through the hospital switchboard had been blocked for the past three days since he had been assigned to a room. He was due to be discharged at noon and was allowed to finally take phone calls. It was Jerome. "Dr. Hamm, how are you feeling?"

"I've got a few cobwebs in my brain, but I seem to be coming around. They're discharging me in a little while."

"That's great. You've got my number so just ring it when you're in the elevator. I'll be waiting outside the entrance. You will talk to me about my friend, won't you?"

"They want me to rest, so I don't know, Jerome."

"I happen to have a friend with a brand new cab who won't be licensed for the next few days. I have exclusive use of his services for the time being. Just look for a Lexus out in front of the hospital when they wheel you down."

"It should be around noon. Does that work for you?"

"Sure. I've got nothing going on right now besides trying to patch up a relationship that I may have blown."

"Oh, what happened?"

"I made a transfer between branes and she happened to make it with me."

"Happened to? I'm sure there's more to it than that, Jerome."

"Alright. I admit I did a very foolish thing."

"Jerome, we need to talk about a few things. You can call me at my home, but I told you I won't be having office hours for a while."

"What's your home number?" asked Jerome.

"My cell number is 212-555-3186," said Hamm.

"I know I blew it with the girl, Dr. Hamm. I won't do anything like that again."

"Do you realize the seriousness of your actions?"

"I said I did."

"I'm not sure you understand, Jerome. What you did was an abduction of the most grievous order. There may be some psychological damage to your friend's psyche. That was a very reckless thing to do."

"I said I blew it, Dr. Hamm. I know what I did was wrong. I'm going to try to make it up to her."

"Don't be surprised if she refuses to see you. As far as your friend is concerned, you are a very dangerous man, Jerome."

"Maybe you could talk to her."

"I don't think that would be wise."

"OK, let's just drop it for now. Just wait for my call."

"I'll be waiting," said Jerome.

Chapter Fourteen

As soon as Dr. Hamm hung up the phone, the door to his room opened and two men in dark suits appeared at his bedside. The younger looking of the two had an earpiece with a wire attached that disappeared into the collar of his coat. He produced a billfold displaying his identification as an operative of The National Security Agency. Although the older man was the first to speak, he produced no identification. "Dr. Hamm, my name is William Conlan, and I'm here to ask you a few questions about one of your patients."

"Jerome Cleveland," said Hamm.

"So, you were expecting a visit from us, is that what you're saying?"

"Of course, not," said the doctor, "I don't imagine anyone ever expects a visit from you people. You no doubt count on putting the subjects of your investigations off by employing the element of surprise."

"You, Doctor, are not the subject of our investigation. Your patient is."

"Do you suspect him of a crime?"

"Not necessarily."

"Perhaps he is involved in some kind of terrorist plot," said Hamm forcing the issue.

"I sense some kind of hostility in you, Dr. Hamm. Is there some reason why you are reluctant to talk to us?"

"Not at all. I'm just busy at the moment. I'm due to be released from this hospital shortly and I need to get dressed." Hamm began peeling the surgical tape off his wrist in order to free his IV port for extraction from the vein on the back of his hand. Normally, this would only be done by the discharge nurse just prior to placing the patient in a wheelchair for departure. Hamm was driving home the point that he was himself a doctor and had control of the situation. Conlan continued his power play, "Can you talk while you get dressed, Doctor, or should we make arrangements to continue this discussion at another venue?"

"Let me guess," said Hamm, "some dark room beneath a bright spotlight."

The younger of the two agents folded his arms across his chest. His body language spoke to the fact that he had witnessed similar verbal exchanges with the senior agent, Conlan, many times in the past and expected the subject to eventually fold under the pressure. What he didn't count on was that Dr. Hamm was well aware of his rights and probably knew the salient elements of The Constitution better than both of them.

"Or maybe we could break you down with the good cop bad cop routine, is that it? Look, Doctor, there's no reason why this has to be difficult. We're just trying to gather some information about Dr. Cleveland."

"Then you know he is a doctor of physics."

"That's right, a PHD in particle physics."

"Then you know as much about him as I do."

"Come now, doctor, as his analyst, you must know a great deal about his personality."

"You don't expect me to betray my doctor patient confidentiality code, do you?"

"I don't care if he hates his mother and clucks like a chicken under hypnosis, Dr. Hamm. In fact, I don't give a rat's ass about any of Cleveland's psychological problems. My job is to care for the security of this country period."

"What makes you think Dr. Cleveland *has* any kind of psychological problems?" asked Hamm. "You indicated that he hasn't committed any crime that you know of . . ."

"That's right. That we know of."

"Then why are you interested in him at all?"

"He was recorded on a surveillance camera at a Bank of America on Seventh Avenue two days ago."

"Did he rob the bank?"

"He claimed to be an amnesia victim and quickly fled the scene when a security guard approached him."

"Is that a crime?"

"No, that is suspicious behavior."

"I think I might do the same thing in his situation. He was merely frightened. Why has he caught the attention of the NSA?"

"He disappeared from your accident scene. He was suddenly gone without a trace for over a week until he was caught on tape. I think you are well aware of his situation because he was also caught on the surveillance tapes at this hospital. We know that he visited this room."

"Yes, he came to wish me a fast recovery. I think that was very nice of him, don't you?"

"Yeah, he's a swell guy, Doctor. But the real reason we are here at all is because that isn't his only disappearing act. He was also caught on a jewelry store surveillance camera on 57th Street. One moment he's there and the next he's gone." Conlan snapped his fingers, "Just like that. Up in smoke."

"There was smoke?"

"That's merely an expression, Dr. Hamm. There wasn't any actual smoke. No sound, no nothing. Just . . . gone."

"Perhaps the camera was faulty," said Hamm.

"The camera is fine. Do you realize the implication of Dr. Cleveland's disappearing act?"

"He's a magician?"

"I don't think so."

"Then how to you explain it, Mr. Conlan?"

"It's not magic, Doctor, we believe it's science."

"You think he invented some kind of way to disappear?"

"We don't really know. But we think that you may," said Conlan pointedly.

"I have no idea what you mean. Now if you will excuse me, I need to get dressed," said Hamm getting out of bed. Conlan blocked his access to the closet in the corner by standing in front of him. Hamm asked him, "Are you arresting me, Mr. Conlan?"

"Not at this time, Doctor."

"Then step out of the way and let me get my clothes."

Conlan did so and then asked, "Have you made arrangements for a ride home?"

That was the moment when it became clear to Dr. Hamm that his telephone conversation with Jerome had been compromised.

"No, I haven't," he lied knowing that Conlan knew it. His phone was bugged and probably his room as well. He needed to call Jerome, but not for his scheduled ride, but to warn him of being in the sights of the NSA. He retrieved his clothes and made a point of moving across the room while ignoring the two men and entered the bathroom. His cell phone was in his pants pocket. He dialed Jerome's cell phone number and was switched to voice mail. He cursed silently and decided to leave a message anyway while flushing the toilet. He whispered forcefully into the phone, "Jerome. Stay away from the hospital! The NSA is here dogging you. Whatever you do, stay away from the hospital and get another phone!"

When he emerged from the bathroom, Conlan gave a smirking glance to his fellow agent and said, "Perhaps you need to get a new phone as well, Dr. Hamm."

"Nice try, Mr. Conlan. You had no idea that I had a cell phone."

"I thought you knew, Doctor," said Conlan.

"Knew what?" asked Hamm.

"The NSA records all emails and cell phone conversations. They've been doing so for the last ten years."

"Would you mind calling me a cab on your way out," said Hamm.

"We don't work for you, Dr. Hamm. Call it yourself," said Conlan as the two men left the room.

~

When Jerome listened to his message from Dr. Hamm on his voicemail, the first thing he did was smash his cell phone. He said under his breath, "God damn suits have a one track mind."

"What?" asked Kamal who overheard him.

"I got a voicemail from Dr. Hamm. He said the authorities are looking for me. He said to stay away from the hospital and get a new cell phone."

"What authorities?"

"The NSA. You know, dark suits, navy blue, Crown Victoria sedans. You can spot them a mile away."

"I knew this shit was going to happen, Jerome," said Kamal. "Somebody saw you disappear and now you're armed and dangerous."

"What do you mean armed?"

"You said it yourself. All suits think the same. They have a one track mind; everything is a weapon to them. The minute anybody invents anything at all, the first thing they do is find out how they can use it to kill somebody."

"You think I would become some kind of secret assassin?" asked Hamm.

"Not you, but somebody. Imagine if some of those black-ops spooks could do what you do?"

"They would die, eventually. I told you the transfers are killing me. My stomach is really off now. I'll bet that Cookie isn't feeling all that great either."

"I can't believe you did that to her," said Kamal. "That's so irresponsible. You could have killed her."

101

"I know, Kamal. I said I won't do it again. I'm not even going to do it myself anymore. One of these times it really would kill me. I'm done traveling between dimensions. But I need to disappear in another sense."

"They probably don't know about the Lexus yet. I could drive you somewhere, maybe some other state."

"That might work, but first things first. I need to find Cookie and see if she is alright."

"Alright, let's drive through the park. If we don't see her, I'll drop you off and you can cross the meadow on foot."

"Sounds like a good plan. What can I say to her to make her forgive me?"

"Just tell the truth."

"I'm not sure I know the truth. I'm not sure why I grabbed her and took her to D-9 in the first place."

"I'm sure," said Kamal.

"What?" asked Jerome.

"It'll come to you."

"No, tell me, Kamal. Why do you think I did it?"

"Because you're in love with her and you knew you didn't have a chance. Not the stuffy Dr. Jerome Cleveland who studies particle physics and goes to symposiums. You had to show her some other Jerome Cleveland. Someone magical."

"How could I be in love with her, Kamal? I just met her three days ago."

"It'll come to you. Trust me."

~

102

Chapter Fifteen

After two trips through the park in Kamal's Lexus, there was still no sight of Cookie. Kamal suggested that he drive Jerome to a new city and then contact Cookie at a later time at her home. He could deliver any message that Jerome wanted in person and thereby avoid any phone conversations. Jerome would have none of it. He refused Kamal's idea saying that the only way to reconcile his relationship was in person and as soon as possible. Kamal reluctantly agreed to Jerome's original plan and left him out at the park's entrance to Sheep Meadow. He walked in a straight line across the meadow until he reached the huge rock situated at the very center. It was a popular meeting place for picnickers and musicians wanting to jam or just laying out in the sun on a nice day. It was not a nice day in Jerome's opinion. Until he could find Cookie and repair the damage he had done to her trust, there would be no nice days ahead.

Just as he reached the large rock in the middle of the meadow, he was startled by a voice behind him, "Hey, Magic Man, just where the hell is my dog?"

Jerome turned and saw Art the juggler walking up behind him. He appeared to be under a great deal of stress as he said, "I need my dog, man. He's not only my dog, but he's my partner. I appreciate you juicing the basket the other day. When you left that fifty, I got a few twenties as well during that show. I owe you one, but that doesn't mean you can mess with my dog."

"I have no idea what you're talking about, Art," said Jerome.

"The gag, man. I know you taught it to Cookie. I saw her when she did the deed and she took Roadie with her."

"You saw Cookie? Where, Art."

"She was right here sitting on the rock, man. Roadie was in her lap licking her face. I was about to call him when a Frisbee flew up and hit me in the ass. I turned around and threw it back to this guy I know who was playing with his Springer, and when I turned back around, she was gone. I called out her name and Roadie's too, but no dice. She couldn't have left the meadow that fast even if she had a helicopter man, and that's when it hit me. You taught Cookie the gag. Let me tell you, she's great at it. One minute she's there and the next, poof!"

"Are you saying that Cookie disappeared right in front of you, Art?"

"Come on, man. Don't play dumb with me. It's a great gag and I don't expect you to tell me how you do it, but I need Roadie back."

"Art, I didn't teach Cookie any magic trick. I don't even know any magic to teach her. It's all been a big misunderstanding."

"Look, man. Your secret's safe with me. All I care about is the dog, OK?"

"I wish I could help you, Art, but I can't."

"You don't want to fuck with me, man. I'm connected to all the gags in this damn city. I could make your life a living hell."

"Get in line, Art. My life is already a living hell. I'll tell you the truth about what is going on, but I need your silence in a big way. I'm afraid the suits are after me."

"What, you some kind of spy or something?"

"No, Art, that's exactly what I'm not. They just think that I am."

"You better start at the beginning, man, and no bullshit, you hear me?"

"No bullshit, I hear you."

Jerome filled Art in on every detail of the last two weeks as well as he could recall them. Art listened quietly, and when Jerome had finished he just sat there and shook his head. After a few minutes, he said, "Man, now I know why the spooks are after you. I called you the bomb before, but you are the Atom Bomb, man. You are one dangerous MO FO! You are the nuclear dude. I thought you just had a good gag. Now I know that it's no gag, and I don't even want to know you. I'm surprised Cookie does. She must not be thinking straight."

"I told you, it wasn't her choice, Art. I pulled a fast one on her. And as far as her traveling between dimensions is concerned, it's nothing that I taught her. Maybe she just picked it up through osmosis on the molecular level."

"And now what about Roadie?" asked Art. "Is he going to start winking in and out right during my act? Just how long do you think that could go on before some spook comes up and dognaps him?"

"I'm sorry, Art. I wish I could make this all go away, but I can't."

"You better make it go away, or I'll make *you* go away . . . permanently! Got it?"

It was then that they saw Conlan and his partner entering Sheep Meadow on foot. Jerome wondered why they didn't have ATV's. He imagined that a helicopter would arrive on the scene shortly, and he told Art that if he wanted to see Cookie and Roadie again, he needed to run interference with the agents who were closing in on them. Fortunately, Art was well equipped for just such a scenario. He gave a hand signal that was nearly invisible and then a short whistle. Jerome realized at that moment that they were not alone. They had been observed the whole time by members of a network who existed just below the surface of the observation of others. Jerome had no clue who they were, but he was sure that Art had the situation well in hand. All of a sudden, the man throwing the Frisbee to the Springer spaniel gave a short command, and the dog immediately took off for the far side of the huge rock and started to bark. His bark was answered by more dogs barking and soon there were more than a dozen of them circling the rock in a fast frenzy. Frisbees began to fill the air around them and soon there was a maelstrom of whirling plastic disks and paws pounding the Earth beneath them. The two agents slowed their pace to the huge rock and re-evaluated their approach. Next, the Frisbees were of a different variety. Frisbee Golf disks began to fill the air as well. They had lead weights imbedded in them in order to give them more mass for longer throws. They also were more dangerous to the unfortunate bodies who found themselves in their way. More than a dozen Frisbee Golf disks filled the air above Art and Jerome as they sat on the rock.

~

Jerry Hamm arrived at his apartment on the upper-west side of Manhattan's Parkside District about twenty minutes after he left Mercy Hospital. If he had binoculars, he could have seen Jerome and Art the gypsy juggler in the middle of Sheep Meadow. As it was he was too tired to concern himself with Jerome's misadventures. He was reluctant to even maintain analysis with Jerome even when he resumed his practice. But there was one thing that was bothering him. During his stay in the hospital, he found himself drifting in and out of consciousness that remained outside the notice of the nursing staff that was monitoring him. But his conversations with Jerome during the non-existent therapy sessions were somehow etched indelibly in his mind. Both he and Jerome had substantiality in his mind alone. The therapy sessions did not really take place. *But why then had Jerome alluded to his patient, Judy Peters, who was being physically abused by her husband William? Where did that information come from? In his mind's verbal exchange with Jerome in his office, while he was actually lying in a coma in Mercy Hospital, he was given information that could not be explained otherwise. Jerome's entity, lodged in his mind, said that Mrs. Peters had a fall. Was that true? Had she actually fallen and attempted to cancel her appointment? Did her husband, William, actually hit her? Was that the origin of her mental unrest and expressions of agoraphobia? Was she just one of the many thousands of women who endured domestic violence and felt helpless to find a remedy for the situation? If that were the case, then clearly he was in denial of the sad elements of her life. Could an analyst be in denial of the myriad of tells regarding a patient crying out for help? He needed to talk to Jerome, as well as Judy Peters. And what about Allison? Did she really go down to Florida to join her friends on Spring Break? How could Jerome have access to that information? None of it made any sense where Jerome was concerned. In his heart, he knew that that less exposure he had with Jerome was for the better. He cared for him as a person, but was very leery of the dangerous scenarios that he could be drawn into. The one thing that frightened him most of all was Jerome's complaint of stomach ailments. He had a sneaking suspicion that when Jerome made the transfer between dimensions, the bacteria in his stomach linings did not make the transfer back. Perhaps it was as simple as having his primary physician prescribe a pro-biotic compound to reintroduce the bacteria. But perhaps it was something much more serious. Perhaps man was not meant to travel between dimensions, and there was a natural safeguard in place to prevent that occurrence.*

~

Cookie was sitting on the rock at the center of Sheep Meadow. She held Roadie in her arms and noticed a cloud cover that was not there a moment before. The weather can't change that fast, she reasoned. What the hell is going on here. Just then, an English pointer named Claire who she knew well bounded up onto the rock. She was about to pet Claire as she had done hundreds of times before, when the dog passed right through her and Roadie to the other side of the rock. Cookie screamed. Roadie barked and shivered in her arms. Apparently the dog knew that there was something otherworldly about Claire's passage through them in their present dimensional strings. Claire's strings were attached to an entirely different brane, and nothing they could do or say would affect her from their side of the universe. They both had never felt so alone. Cookie wanted Jerome to come and lead her back to her home dimension. Roadie missed Art the gypsy and whimpered miserably in Cookie's arms. Feeling the frightened state of the animal awoke a protective instinct that gave her strength. She told Roadie, "Don't worry, Sweetie, we're going to beat this thing. We're going home soon. Just hang on to your Aunt Cookie and everything's going to be fine."

Roadie licked her face.

~

Kamal's Lexus was making another turn across the park on Terrace drive when he spotted the suits closing in on Jerome and Art the gypsy. He decided that desperate times call for desperate action. He jumped the curb and headed the Lexus across Sheep Meadow toward the huge rock. When he came near to the two men, his car was pummeled by Frisbees that he knew were making a series of ugly marks in the paint of his fine automobile. He didn't care in the least because he knew the car had been compromised. There was no other explanation for the agents zeroing in on Jerome so quickly. His so-called friend, who was a Lexus dealer in Fort Lee, New Jersey, had sold him out. There was undoubtedly a tracking device somewhere within the car. He would lose the car as soon as he could deliver Jerome to a safe place. He would miss the car, but there would be other cars. The most important issue at hand, as he saw it, was that there would be other days as well. Better days away from the trials of the transparent patient who spiraled his otherwise uneventful life into a mess of unbelievable complications.

When he skidded to a stop at the rock, Jerome and Art jumped in the Lexus before the two agents could react. They were still fending off the Frisbees coming at them from all angles. Jerome said to Kamal, "Right on time, Buddy. Hit it!"

Kamal raced away from the center of Sheep Meadow at sixty miles an hour. His tires screeched when he reached the pavement of East Drive and he turned South and ran four blocks to 65th Street to exit the park. Jerome told him, "We should go back to Cookie's and establish a base of operations. I'm sure that Watson will be on board as soon as he knows the situation."

"But the car's hot," said Kamal.

"What do you mean?" asked Jerome.

"The guy who sold it to us is a shithead, that's what."

"A tracking device?"

"I think so."

"So then don't go to Cookie's, Kamal. Take us to the Met."

"I'm on it," said Kamal. He drove over to 5th Avenue from 65th Street and took a left turn uptown. After seventeen short blocks, he left them at 82nd Street at the front entrance of The Metropolitan Museum of Art. Kamal took off in a screech of tires hoping to place as much distance as he could between Jerome and the tracking device in his car.

~

Art led Jerome through the front entrance of the Met and walked up to the ticket tables on the right side of the lobby.

Admission was free, but patrons were encouraged to make a donation of at least five dollars. He placed a twenty-dollar bill in the basket on the first table and took two wrist ribbons, handing one to Jerome. "Put it on your left wrist, Jerome," he told him.

"We're not actually going to hang around looking at art are we?"

"No, we're heading out the side exit in about two minutes," said Art.

"Then why the donation?" asked Jerome.

"Got to support the arts, man."

The side exit on the south side took them out to 5th Avenue about fifteen blocks north of Cookie's Penthouse condo. They decided to spit up, Art staying back and watching for any sign of the spooks following Jerome. As far as he could tell, they were in the clear. No one was following Jerome, so they had effectively lost their tail. Art followed at a meandering pace constantly stopping and looking back along 5th Avenue for any sign of a dark blue Crown Vic. The Crown Victoria was the car of choice by most of the domestic security agencies like the NSA and Homeland Security. The FBI favored Fords. Art was well aware that the NSA might not be the only agency dogging Jerome. Langley and Quantico were sure to place Jerome in their sights eventually. It was just a matter of time. Jerome desperately needed to disappear permanently, but he needed to make sure that Cookie could make the transfer back from D-9 first. Roadie, too. Art told himself he cared more for Cookie's welfare than Roadie's, but he suspected that it was a lie. Roadie had been with him for over seven years, and he dearly loved the dog.

When Art reached Cookie's condo, Alphonse the concierge, simply motioned for him to go on up. He told him, "Dr. Cleveland has already arrived and said to expect you shortly, Art. What's going on?"

"Nothing that you need to be concerned about, Alphonse. We're not breaking any laws or anything. This is just a logistics meeting of the minds in order to ensure the safety of Ms. Doe."

"Are you sure there isn't anything I can do?"

"As a matter of fact there is; if you happen to see anyone who resembles any kind of government spook, see if you can run a little interference and give us a heads up. Is there a back exit from the building should we need it?"

"There is a freight elevator that will take you to a fire exit. And then, there are always the stairs."

"OK, thanks, Alphonse. Hopefully, we won't need to use either of them."

"Sure you can't tell me what's going on?"

"Trust me, Alphonse. You really don't want to know."

"It's not a kidnapping is it?"

"No, Alphonse. It's definitely not a kidnapping."

"Well then, good luck, Art," said Alphonse as the elevator reached the lobby and the bell sounded.

When Watson opened the door to Cookie's penthouse, the look in his eye seemingly could have burned a hole right through Art the gypsy's head. All he said was, "What the fuck, Art?"

"Jerome didn't say?"

"He didn't say squat. Where is Cookie?"

"We don't exactly know, but we're going to get her back. At least Jerome is."

"I don't like this at all," said Watson. "What do you mean you don't know where she is?"

"Well, we can't see her because she slipped over to the other side."

"What other side?"

"Another dimension. Jerome calls it D-9."

"Well, can't she just slip back?" asked Watson.

"Yeah, that's the idea. And we think she'll do it right here."

"Then what's the problem?"

"It's a little scary."

"Spill it, Art. You know that Cookie is very dear to me."

"Well, there are two of her. Actually, there are two of you as well?"

"What the hell are you talking about, Art?"

"The other dimension, D-9 has a Cookie in it as well. There is also another Watson there, presumably. Jerome says that it might be dangerous for the two of them to meet up."

"What, like an explosion or something? Like matter and antimatter canceling each other out?"

"No, Watson, nothing so violent. But Jerome thinks that it could be really unsettling to her psyche. We all think we are one of a kind. It could be kind of catastrophic to encounter another self in a different universe. Hopefully, that won't happen. We're hoping she can avoid the other Cookie entirely. Our best hope is that she will wait to enter the building until she sees the other Cookie go out."

"What about the other Watson? The other me? Won't he see her?"

"She won't be visible to him. Jerome thinks that only the D-9 Cookie could sense her presence."

"What happened when Jerome encountered his other self?" asked Watson.

"Nothing because the other Jerome had passed over to the other side."

"What other side?"

"Death."

"Oh, this just gets better and better," said Watson sardonically. "What did Cookie ever do to deserve this shit?"

"She was just being Cookie. You know how enchanting she is. Jerome just couldn't resist her charms. He said he couldn't help himself, that he had never met anyone like her before."

"Well, that's just great," said Watson darkly. "Let me tell you, Art, if Jerome doesn't get her back where she belongs, I think I'm going to send him to the other side."

"That's not like you, Watson, you're a pacifist," said Art.

"Yeah, well people change."

~

Chapter Sixteen

Cookie had Roadie in her arms standing on the other side Park Avenue from her condominium. The people passing by obviously made no notice of her because they were living their lives on an entirely different plane. Roadie whimpered, and she knew that it was not because he was hungry. She knew he was missing his best friend, Art. They sat down against the building to wait. After nearly an hour, she saw Jerome enter the lobby of her building. Then, a short time later, Art entered the building as well. When Roadie saw Art, he barked a loud greeting and was confused why Art did not cross the street and take him in his arms. Cookie told him, "Just hold on, sweetie. Art still loves you, he just can't see you right now. Just be patient and I'll get you back to him in a jiffy." Roadie licked her face. Cookie knew they had reasoned it out. She couldn't very well make the transfer in the middle of Sheep Meadow with Roadie without attracting a lot of very dangerous attention, even if she knew how. Slipping back to D-9 was an accident and she wasn't sure she could make it back by herself, but she damned well was going to try. She just had to do it in her own home. She said a small prayer, "Come on, Cookie," she urged her other self, "go on out to get something. Walk over to the meadow and meet with your friends." It was very strange, to say the least, talking silently to herself, hoping that she would do something that she herself might do in that other universe. At last she got her wish. She saw the D-9 Cookie leave the building. She wasted no time crossing the street, walking right through the vehicles without fear, knowing that they could do her no harm in her present plane. She entered the lobby and walked through the door of the stairway holding Roadie at her side. She had to climb seven flights of stairs, something that she had never had to do before. But she was not able to call the elevator to the lobby. She knew that her finger would pass impotently right through the lighted button. When she reached the seventh floor, she stopped to catch her breath. Finally she walked through the front door, not bothering to actually open it, and paused to detect the presence of anyone in the apartment. It appeared to be empty. There was no sign of Watson at all. He might have traveled over to Brooklyn to visit his sister, which he often did when Cookie had no need for his services. At any rate, she was both pleased and sorry to find herself alone in her apartment. She had never been so alone in her life. She knew that Roadie was feeling the same way. She walked into the library.

~

In the other library on an entirely different brane were Watson, Art and Jerome Cleveland putting their heads together in order to come up with a course of action. Jerome suggested, "She may actually be here already. She might actually be able to see us although she can't interact."

Cookie screamed at them from the brane of strings in D-9, "Yes, Jerome, I'm here. You're right I am here even though I know you can't see me. Bring me back, Jerome! Please, bring Roadie and me back to the other side!"

Watson then said, "So, let's say she's here, right in this room, how do you intend to bring her back?"

"I'm not sure. I could try to travel to D-9, but I'd like to try something else first."

"Don't screw around, Jerome. You are the cause of all this shit. You have a responsibility to make things right."

"I promise, I'll do everything I can, but just bear with me for a moment. I'm going to try to talk her over to this side."

"What do you mean talk her over?" asked Watson hotly. "Quit stalling!"

"Just listen, Watson. This might work. If it doesn't, I'll go to her and bring her back with me."

"Well, go ahead," said Art. "Hang on, buddy, daddy's right here," he promised even though he knew that Roadie couldn't hear him.

"Cookie!" began Jerome, "you can do this. You can make the transfer between the dimensions. Think back what were you saying or doing when you went over to D-9. Think exactly what you were doing and thinking. Say it out loud if it will help you remember. I know you can do it. But one thing to remember, make sure you have a good hold of Roadie when you make the transfer."

Cookie heard Jerome's words clearly. She knew that meant that she still had a strong connection to the other side, the original side where she belongs. She began to talk to herself out loud, *Come on Cookie, what were you doing? You were sitting on the rock in the middle of Sheep Meadow. Roadie was sitting in your lap and licking your face. His tongue felt like sandpaper and was rough on your skin. You asked him to stop. He wouldn't stop licking and you*

117

closed your eyes very tightly and you commanded him forcefully, STOP IT ROADIE! GET OUT OF HERE. GET OUT OF HERE! And then they suddenly both slipped out of their dimensional plane and materialized in what Jerome called D-9. Cookie tried to repeat her actions as closely as she could remember. She said to the dog, "Go ahead now, Roadie, lick my face again. Like my face with your sandpaper tongue!" Roadie began to lick her face when she held him up to her breast. He licked frantically sensing her urgent plea. When he was licking her very forcefully, she once again closed her eyes very tightly and shouted, STOP IT, ROADIE! GET OUT OF HERE! GET OUT OF HERE!"

A silver shimmering light enveloped Cookie and the dog and they immediately made the transfer back to their original dimension. When she knew that the three men could see her, tears began to fill her eyes. Jerome was afraid that she would hate him for what he had done to her, all the trouble he had caused and the danger that he put her in. He braced himself for her attack. She ran to him and threw herself into his arms. Roadie threw himself into Art's arms as well. Cookie said between sobs, "Oh, Jerome. I was so alone. I don't ever want to be that alone again. Hold me Jerome. Don't ever let me go."

~

Alphonse rang up Cookie's apartment with some bad news. "Watson, Art told me to be on the lookout for some spooky characters who might want to talk to Cookie."

"And?" asked Watson.

"I got rid of them. No warrant, they were just fishing. But what do you want to bet the next time they come they'll have one. Possibly an arrest warrant with both of your names on it."

"You did well, Alphonse. Just cooperate with them when they return. Hopefully, we won't be here."

Watson hung up the phone and told the others, "They've made the connection to Cookie somehow. You weren't tailed here, were you, Art?"

"No, I would have spotted a tail."

"And Kamal's car is nowhere in the area. What are these guys psychic or something?" asked Jerome.

"No, maybe they're just lucky. Alphonse said they were just fishing. Maybe that's all there was to it. They made Art by his face recognition at the park, and it's no great feat to connect him to Cookie. He's here all the time. Maybe they don't have enough probability for a warrant," said Watson.

"Let's hope not," said Cookie. "But the fact remains that Jerome is public enemy number one, and none of us want to become number two."

"Cookie's right," said Jerome. "I'm endangering all of you. I have to leave as soon as I can."

"I'm going with you," said Cookie. "At least for the time being."

"It's not safe, Cookie," said Jerome.

"Nowhere is safe, Jerome. I could get mugged tomorrow in the park and maybe not survive. I'll take my chances with you if you'll have me."

"How can you forgive me for what I've gotten you into, Cookie?"

"Life has no guarantees, Jerome. Who's to say what I'm supposed to be doing with my life? I've been stagnated here lately, no offense guys," she motioned to Watson and Art, "but I've known all along that my life has to stand for something more than hanging out at the park and going to the Met."

"What did your parents want you to do?" asked Jerome.

"What difference does it make, they're ancient history."

"No, seriously, did they send you to school?"

"Cookie's an artist," said Watson. "Maybe the most gifted artist of her generation, but there is just one problem."

"What's that," asked Jerome.

"She doesn't paint."

"Why have you given up on your art, Cookie?" asked Jerome.

"There's just no point to it. Lord knows I don't need the money. And I never really wanted the attention."

"But you're abandoning your gift. It's like throwing it back in the face of the creator."

"So what do you expect me to do? If I put together a portfolio, how are we going to avoid the spooks who are bird-dogging you?"

"You'll just have to do it without me," said Jerome.

"Then you don't want me," said Cookie.

"No, Cookie, you're wrong. I want you more than anything. I just think that I'm poison for you. For all of you, for that matter."

"Why don't you let us decide who is poison and who isn't," said Art. "No spook is going to tell me who I can and can't have for a friend."

"OK, but let's deal with the issue at hand. I have to make an exit from this apartment unobserved. How do we manage that?"

"Kamal will do it," suggested Art. "He's bound to score another set of wheels that the suits aren't connected to."

"I hope you're right," said Jerome. "In the mean time, I'd just like to say how grateful I am for all of you standing by me."

"No problem," said Art. "As far as I'm concerned, you were just what the doctor ordered to give a little spice to our lives."

"I agree," said Watson.

"And I do as well," said Cookie. "I feel like I've been waiting for you to find me for my whole life, Jerome."

"I feel like I'm in some kind of dream," said Jerome. "I just hope I don't ever wake up."

~

Kamal parked three blocks away from Cookies penthouse. He had traded in the Lexus back in Fort Lee making sure his so called "friend" knew that he was wise to him, and that the issue of being sold out to the feds was far from over. He went to another dealer and found the most non-descript vehicle he could think of. It was a Jeep Cherokee that needed a new paint job, but seemed to be mechanically sound. Alphonse called up to the apartment and was told to send Kamal on up. Kamal greeted them warmly in the library and related the particulars of his day regarding the transfer of vehicles. He gratefully accepted a snifter of very expensive brandy from Cookie's wet bar. It had been a long day.

"It's good to see you back in Kansas, Dorothy," said Kamal. "Toto, too."

They all laughed at Kamal's allusion to The Wizard of Oz. Watson then nodded toward Jerome and said, "Pay no attention to the man behind the curtain." That brought another round of laughter. It was sorely needed release of tension. But there was an unsaid issue that they all were aware of and needed to address. Whether or not it was actually the case, they appeared to be in danger of resembling some kind of terrorist cell and attracting the attention of the NSA and The Department of Homeland Security. Cookie suggested that they all lay low for a while and take the time to germinate an effective plan. Number one: Jerome had to relocate. Number two: Cookie wanted to join him once his new life was in order. Number three: His account in Partners with Geneva had to be closed and transferred offshore, preferably to the Cayman Islands. Number four: all the people in the room besides Cookie had to be prepared to say goodbye to Jerome for the last time. There was no reasonable way to keep in touch with each other without attracting the attention of the spooks who wanted Jerome's discovery to use as a weapon.

~

Chapter Seventeen

Dr. Hamm was resting quietly in his home when Agent Conlan and his partner came to call. There was no doorman in his apartment at 89th Street and Central Park West, so he learned of their arrival by the knock on his door.

"Agent Conlan, what a nice surprise," said Jerry Hamm sarcastically.

"Look, I'm sorry about our last encounter, Dr. Hamm, we're not really the bad guys. We're just trying to clean up some mysteries for our employers. They are very powerful men, blah blah blah, and they don't much like mysteries."

"Good for them."

"So, if you wouldn't mind, Doctor, would you please give us the address of your patient named Jerome Cleveland?"

"Love to," he said exasperatedly. "Especially if it will get you off my back. His address is the St, Moritz Hotel on 59th Street. It's by the park entrance, right next to the Plaza Hotel."

"That's all you have to give us?" asked Conlan.

"That's more than I'm required of by law, Inspector. Let me assure you, I acquiesce only because it would serve no one to stall the inevitable progression of your investigation. You will no doubt learn all that I know about Jerome Cleveland, and I encourage you to do so. He is a fine man, and a patriot. Is there some other way I can help you?" asked Hamm.

"A room number perhaps? How about a next of kin or someone to advise in the case of emergency? Do your files on your patients include that?"

"Now I'm sure you're treading on the rights of my patient. You have his name, you have his address, you can call on him yourself."

"You know we won't find him at the St. Moritz," said Conlan.

"I am not a psychic, Inspector, I can't tell you what you will, or what you will not find."

"Thanks again for your cooperation, Dr. Hamm," Conlan said in his best, menacing suit-in-your-face, dripping sarcastic voice.

"Any time," said Hamm closing the door, *Asshole,* he wisely didn't add but said to himself.

~

Jerome and Kamal left Cookie's apartment and made their way back to the Jeep Cherokee parked three streets over on 2nd Ave. and E. 85th Street. They looked the vehicle over from bumper to bumper and found no evidence of tampering, but decided not to trust it for the time being. They then started out on foot in the direction of Jerome's brownstone apartment up in Harlem. They would hole up for surveillance nearby and watch for an hour or so to spot a recurrent circling of a familiar vehicle. If they found none, they would chance entering Kamal's next door apartment and leave Jerome's untouched. Jerome figured that the spooks could easily do a search for recently rented or purchased properties in his name and set up an ambush. Fortunately, their paranoia was unfounded as they remained unmolested and unobserved as far as they could tell. When they entered Kamal's apartment, they found it just the way Kamal had left it, which was completely empty. He had yet to move any furniture in or even place any food in the cupboards or refrigerator. There was literally no place inside the apartment where a listening device or camera could be placed. The air-conditioning vents on the floor appeared to be empty of any listening hardware, and a camera placed there would be useless showing only the ceiling above. They felt confident they could set up a base of operations for a short while before leaving town. Jerome had purchased a half-dozen disposable cell phones and dialed Cookie's number on one of them. Watson answered on the first ring with one of the half-dozen he had given him, "You have reached the rabbit hole," he answered facetiously.

"Mad Hatter here," said Jerome with equal jocular emphasis, "Tweedle-Dee is standing by as well," referring to Kamal standing next to him.

"How long do we have before your friends triangulate either your or our location, Jerome?" asked Watson.

"I have no idea. But just to be safe, trash the phone when I hang up."

"I will. Do you need to speak to Cookie?" he asked.

"No, that can wait. Just tell her that I will try to get in contact with Dr. Hamm for a joint session either at his house or in his office."

"What do you have in mind?" asked Watson.

"I'm guessing hypnosis is the answer, Watson. We have to unlearn the ability to slip into dimension nine."

"Just so you know, my promise to you still stands. If you scramble Cookie's brain with any of your hair-brained attempts to set things right . . ."

"I know. You will make me pay dearly for it."

"You can count on it, Jerome."

When he hung up the phone, Kamal asked him, "What was that all about?"

"Just a warning. I fully expected it."

"What kind of warning?"

"He said he'll kick my ass if I get Cookie into any more trouble, physically *or* mentally."

"He'll have to get in line, Jerome. I'll kick your ass first," said Kamal. "I told you she was a friend of mine as well."

"Everybody wants to kick my ass. I can't wait to leave this town," said Jerome.

"You have only yourself to blame. Scientists have a bad habit of asking first and apologizing later."

"I have to admit you're right, Kamal."

Jerome left Kamal's apartment and hailed a cab to the New York Public Library. This time he was able to utilize the research facilities with his corporeal presence intact. After logging on to a computer terminal open to public use, he looked up a directory of physicians in the immediate Manhattan vicinity. He found Hamm's name listed along with his discipline, psychiatry, and a list of awards and publications attributed to him. But there was no listing for his address. He had Dr. Hamm's cell phone number, but that would surely be bugged considering the recent warning that he left on Jerome's earlier cell phone. He knew that when he made a call to

Hamm, they would both have to trash their phones. But there was no other choice as far as he was concerned. He had to make the call and replace Hamm's phone when it was over. He decided that he had to limit the call to one minute. He hoped that would be enough time to arrange a meeting without disclosing where it would take place. Hamm answered as soon as the call went through. Jerome knew he was expecting the call. His next few words were critical. He placed his sleeve over the mouthpiece of the phone and in a gravelly voice said, "This is Bill Peter's you quack son-of-a-bitch. Just where do you get off accusing me of spousal abuse? Where the hell did you hear that load of crap? I can assure you it wasn't from my wife, Judith. Just where did you hear it, wise guy. I'd like to meet you there and kick your sorry ass. Tell me where you heard it!" he said finally, quickly cutting off the call.

He knew that Dr. Hamm would make the connection in time. If he thought back to where he first heard the news that Mr. Peters was hitting his wife, he had only to go there and Jerome would meet up with him. At first he thought it was during a session with Jerome in his office. Then he remembered that Jerome's existence was only manifested in his mind during the time he was in a coma. He had to go back to Mercy Hospital. That was where he first got the news that Mrs. Peters was being abused. *Could it actually be true? Could she have been expressing all the tells of spousal abuse and he was just covering up all the indications with his sense of denial?* He would deal with that at a later time. For now, it was only important to go back to Mercy Hospital and look for Jerome.

~

Chapter Eighteen

Cookie was leaving her apartment a short time later when Conlan and his cohort grabbed her at the curb. They forced her into their Crown Victoria with no explanation or even a wisp of Miranda rights. She had the right to be captive by the spooks and that was the end of the story. The Patriot act was a few weeks short of being repealed and the gloves were still off as far as the National Security Agency was concerned. That was how Dr. Hamm's hospital room phone had been compromised. His cell phone was bugged as well. It was only a short leap to Jerome through his association with Hamm and the subsequent warrant for his arrest after the jewelry shop closed circuit camera caught his disappearing act. As fate would have it, that was Cookie's undoing as well. A camera on the perimeter of Sheep Meadow placed by the local police after a series of muggings in the area caught her winking out accidentally into dimension-nine with a Jack Russell Terrier in her arms. The NSA reviewed the tape several times and could come up with no explanation for her rapid disappearance. Then they made the connection with Jerome Cleveland through his association with the cab driver, Kamal Stanos. Kamal was profiled by the local PD for his association with street performers and the woman known as Cookie Doe.

Cookie didn't scream at the time of her abduction. She was indeed too cool a Cookie for that. She took the opportunity to threaten them instead. "Listen, Dickhead," she began, "I've wanted a hobby lately and guess now whose it? You are, and your friend Barney Rubble as well. After I sue you both for false arrest, I will use all of my considerable power as CEO of a fortune 500 company to make your life a living hell. Doesn't that sound like fun?"

Conlan was unfazed. He apparently had carte blanch authority to step on the rights of others when the question of national security reared its ugly head. Cookie knew that her threats were groundless, but was unable to afford the two men any kind of respect after her rude apprehension. When Conlan grabbed her from behind, she had the distinct impression that he was copping a feel as well.

They took Cookie to a room with a single bed and a chair and locked her inside. There was a single light fixture on the ceiling enclosed by a wire cage should she have the sudden urge to unscrew the bulb and electrocute herself for no apparent reason. An hour and twenty minutes passed until Conlan stuck his ugly mug up to the glass window in the door and smiled at her. She gave him the salute he deserved with a single finger. "Asshole," she mouthed as she knew her voice wouldn't carry out of the room. Then the door opened and a female agent entered the room. She was an attractive redhead with her hair pulled back in a pony tail tied with a black ribbon. She wore a blue blazer like Conlan and had the same white shirt as well. Her mind held the phrase, *"Cookie cutter cops."*

The woman then began, "I'm sorry for the way that Agent Conlan has treated you, Ma'am, can I get you something to drink? Coffee or perhaps a soft drink?"

"Only if it's at The Tavern on the Green," she said referring to the restaurant on the side of Central Park. "When do I get out of here Agent . . . ?"

"I'm Holly Blume," said the agent smiling. "I try not to be as much of a dick as Conlan."

"That should be easy to pull off," said Cookie. "Where does he get off abducting me like some victim in a bad movie? What an asshole move that was. At least he could have questioned me first. I wasn't running away. I was just running out for a latte at Starbucks."

"There seems to be some question about your sudden disappearance from the park. Agent Conlan has been authorized to determine the means of that disappearance," said Blume.

"And what evidence do you have regarding this alleged disappearance?" asked Cookie.

"A surveillance tape on a light pole at the park entrance."

""Obviously, the tape has been doctored, Agent Blume. People don't just disappear."

"No, they don't. But I'm afraid you may have to stay here for a while until this can be straightened out. I can get you some decent food and a change of clothes when you need them."

"So, you're the good cop in the good cop, bad cop scenario, is that it?"

"I'm only as good as my job allows me to be. I'm a patriot, Ms. Doe. That's not a dirty word in my book."

"I'm a patriot as well, Agent Blume. In fact I'm a capitalist. You do know who I am, don't you?"

"I've seen your picture on the bottle, so yes, I know who you are."

"And you know my habits as well I assume."

"Yes, Ms. Doe. I know where you go and with whom you associate."

"All patriots, I assure you."

"That may well be the case, but your tax dollars hire people like me to make sure of it. I'm sure you were in this city when the planes flew into the towers, isn't that so?"

"I was twelve years old. It was horrible," said Cookie sadly.

"Yes, it was, Ms. Doe."

"You can call me Cookie, Agent Blume."

"It's Holly," said the agent. "Yes, it was horrible, Cookie. I was here when it happened, too."

"Did you lose any friends, Holly? I did, and at that moment, I became more of a patriot than I ever was before. So don't question my loyalty to my country, OK?"

"OK, Cookie. But you have to understand that you appear to be a dangerous person according to the tape."

"The tape is fucked up. What can I say?"

"Do you know a man named Jerome Cleveland?"

"Isn't this the part where I ask for a lawyer?"

"You're not charged with any crime, Cookie. We're just asking questions at this point."

"And I don't have to answer them, is that right?"

"That's your choice. But you would be helping your country a great deal if you just cooperate with this agency for the time being."

"OK, I know Jerome Cleveland. Has he committed any crime?"

"That is yet to be determined. I can tell you that he is not very popular among his colleagues."

"Neither am I. I've heard that Mrs. Butterworth can't stand me."

Agent Blume laughed heartily at her remark. It broke some of the tension in the room. Agent Blume then said, "Listen, Cookie, let me put my cards on the table here."

"By all means," said Cookie.

"We think that your friend Jerome has developed some kind of way to bend light in a way that makes objects invisible. If this is true, there are some factions in other countries who would really like to get their hands on the process. We feel it is in our best interest to protect Dr. Cleveland from that eventuality."

"Eventuality? So you are convinced that Jerome isn't capable of taking care of himself?"

"The bad guys are really bad, Cookie. They don't regard human life the same way we do."

"So if Jerome had this procedure and someone tried to attack him, why wouldn't he just become invisible, Holly? It seems to me that he is a lot more capable than you are of protecting himself."

"He has in fact done just that," said Blume. "We are trying to find him after his last disappearance."

"When did that happen?" asked Cookie.

"Actually, it was by car. A car traversed Sheep Meadow even though there are no roads that go through it. A car spirited Dr. Cleveland and a friend of yours away from Center Rock as Agents Conlan and Arnold were closing in on them."

"And you have no idea where he is now?" asked Cookie.

"That is correct, we don't"

"Well, neither do I," she said truthfully. "Get out your polygraph and let's get this thing over with."

"You know you don't have to submit to a polygraph, Cookie, but you're still willing to take one?"

"You bet," said Cookie.

"That won't be necessary. Just give me a few minutes to cross a few t's and dot some i's. I think you'll be able to leave in a few minutes."

"That's it? No apologies?"

"You've gotten one from me, Cookie. I'm afraid Agent Conlan thinks he has a really big dick."

"I think he really *is* a big dick."

"Just between the two of us, so do I," said Agent Blume.

~

Dr. Hamm spotted Jerome sitting in the front passenger seat of a Jeep Cherokee parked in front of Mercy Hospital. There was a dark haired man with a large mustache in the driver's seat. He quickly approached the car and opened the rear driver's-side door, "How about a ride, fella's?" he asked.

"Get in," said Kamal.

Hamm got in the back seat and closed the door. Kamal then pulled out of the parking spot and cruised away from the hospital grounds. Jerome wasted no time in asking, "What about hypnosis, Jerry. Can you erase the procedure from our minds?"

"Our minds?" questioned Hamm. "Have you got a mouse in your pocket?"

"The girl I told you about. She passed through on her own accidentally. I think it can happen again at any time. Do you think you can help?"

"We've got to try something, Jerome. What about your research? Are you willing to lose that as well?"

"I don't have a choice, Jerry. The passage to D-9 has been wreaking havoc with my internal organs. The next time might kill me. Maybe our strings just aren't supposed to travel away from this brane. One dimension is enough for this universe."

"But is one universe enough?" asked Hamm.

"That's another question for another time. When can you meet with Cookie to take her under?"

"Cookie?" asked Hamm.

"That's her name. When can you erase the procedure from her memory?"

"As soon as you can take her to my office, Jerome. I agree that time is of the essence. She could make the passage again at any time if she indeed did it accidentally."

"OK, we'll drop you off at your office. Give us about an hour to locate Cookie and bring her there."

~

After Jerome and Kamal found Cookie and brought her to Dr. Hamm's office. They left for the time being to tie up some loose ends with the brownstone up in Harlem. Jerome made arrangements to rent out his half of the duplex with instructions that the Realtor was to deliver the proceeds to Kamal. Then Jerome asked Kamal to take him to the Port Authority building to pick up some train schedules to plan his exodus out of the city. After waiting thirty minutes at the curb, Kamal finally realized what had happened. It would be a full five weeks before Kamal would again see Jerome Cleveland in New York City.

~

Cookie sat on Hamm's couch expressing an outward calm she didn't feel. Hamm asked her knowingly, "Are you nervous, Ms. Doe?"

"Why would you ask that?" she said avoiding the question with one of her own.

"Why are you reluctant to answer my simple question?" he asked.

"Do you think we could set some kind of record for questions asked in a row?"

"Are you interested in setting records?" asked Hamm suppressing a chuckle.

"Do many of your patients set records?" asked Cookie.

"Are you speaking of Dr. Cleveland?" he asked her and couldn't help laughing this time. "I have to say, this is a most interesting dialogue as a precursor to a therapy session, Ms. Doe."

"Aha, you broke the pattern, Dr. Hamm. That wasn't a question," said Cookie.

"I guess you win," said Hamm.

"How about a staring contest. I'll bet I can make you blink first."

"I don't doubt it, Ms. Doe."

"Please call me Cookie."

"Alright."

"And I should call you . . .?"

"Dr. Hamm," he said soberly.

"Well, now that we've gotten that out of the way, Dr. Hamm," she said forcefully.

"I want you to stay focused on our objective, Cookie. This is very important."

"I know how important it is, Dr. Hamm. And yes, I'm nervous. Nervous as hell."

"Interesting choice of words, Cookie. What do you think about hell?"

"I try not to think about it."

"And D-9? What do you think about the place where Dr. Cleveland took you?"

"I know what you're getting at. I suppose that if there is a hell on Earth, D-9 is as good a candidate as any other."

"Pretty scary, huh?"

"You have no idea," she said seriously.

"No, Cookie, I don't. Nor do I have any wish to. Nobody should experience that reality in my opinion."

"If it *is* a reality, it's certainly *not ours*," said Cookie.

"No, it isn't. It's an abomination. A place that shouldn't exist at all, but it does."

"Thanks to Jerome," said Cookie.

"Yes, unfortunately, thanks to Dr. Cleveland."

"Why can't you call him Jerome? I thought he was a friend of yours."

"Yes, he is a friend."

"Why are you so formal, Dr. Hamm?"

"It's my job to be formal, Ms. Doe."

"So now it's not Cookie."

"I would rather address you as Ms. Doe. Does that make you uncomfortable?"

"Is there someplace I'd rather be? You betcha'."

"This is where you need to be, Ms. Doe. With any luck, I'm going to save your life."

"Luck?"

"There are no guarantees, Ms. Doe. I'm going to try to suppress a memory or yours. It is not foolproof. There are many pathways into your mind and memories. I have to divert all of them for you to become safe."

"Safe from what?" asked Cookie.

"From damaging your internal organs."

"I know I've lost my appetite, but I thought that was just part of the excitement."

"Yes, it is excitement," said Hamm. "Your insides are excited as far as I can determine. But that in itself is a very dangerous thing. Think about it like this: a microwave excites the water molecules in the substances placed in them. They speed up and become hot. In your case, it is not heat, but static position in space. You are moving too fast for your own good when you travel to D-9."

"I've only done it twice, Dr. Hamm."

"Two times too many," said the doctor. "The next time might damage your organs permanently."

"How do you know? This is totally new ground, is it not?"

"Oppenheimer broke new ground, Ms. Doe. There are about a half-million Japanese people that are sorry that he did."

"The bomb? That's a little dramatic, isn't it?"

"Yes, it is, but it is also an entirely appropriate analogy. You and your friend Dr. Cleveland have been playing a very dangerous game."

"So, let's get on with it. If you're going to save my life, save away."

"I need your complete trust, Ms. Doe."

"It would help if you call me Cookie."

"I need your complete trust, Cookie."

"Alright . . . ?"

"Jerry. You may call me Jerry, Cookie, but I need you to stay focused on how important this session is for your well being."

"I'll stay focused. I want to forget all about D-9 and how to get there."

"And how do you feel about Dr. Cleveland?"

"Jerome? I'm in love with Jerome."

"Well, that may become a problem with your therapy."

"What are you talking about?"

"Remember me talking about the many pathways, or inroads if you will, to your subconscious mind?"

"Yes, what about them."

"You friend, Jerome is one of them."

"What are you saying?"

"You may have to lose all conscious memory of your friend, Cookie."

"What do you mean conscious memory? What other kind of memory is there?"

"You have a series of synaptic connections with your experiences with Dr. Cleveland. In order to break those connections, it may be necessary to forget any semblance of your relationship. But there is always the possibility of meeting Dr. Cleveland again. You could fall in love all over again, but without the dangerous inroads of your connection to D-9."

"You really don't know what the hell you're talking about, do you, Dr. Hamm?"

"I thought it was Jerry at this point."

"Whatever. You've never done this before, have you, Jerry?" asked Cookie with heat in her voice for the first time.

"Look, Cookie, I won't lie to you. No, I've never suppressed anyone's memory to this extent. This is dangerous ground, therapeutically speaking. It is not encouraged because of potential side effects."

"Oh, swell, what kind of side effects, Doctor?"

"You could lose something more than your memory of Dr. Cleveland. A gift, for instance. What if you were to lose the ability to, say, play the violin?"

"I can't play the violin."

"That was just an example. I'm sure you are gifted in other ways, Cookie."

"I was a painter. Some people say I should return to it."

"And so you may," said Hamm. "I just want you to be aware of the risks with the procedure I have in mind for you."

"Hypnosis, right?"

"As well as medication for the short term. A psychotropic solution used to treat PTSD."

"Scrambled brains for breakfast, is that it?"

"Nothing so dramatic. You may appear to be laconic for a short while. Nothing more severe than that."

"And I will lose all memory of the man I love."

"Yes, I'm afraid so."

"Well, forget it," said Cookie forcefully standing up from the couch and heading for the door."

"Cookie wait!" urged Hamm. "You don't know what you're getting into. The state you're in could trigger another episode of transfer to D-9 without your control."

"I'll chance it, Jerry," she said emphasizing the use of his given name. She was all but dismissing his position as physician and stating for the record she only considered him a layman for the time being. The outer door to his treatment room closed behind her driving home the point.

~

Chapter Nineteen

When Cookie reached the curbside of Hamm's downtown office, she spotted Kamal behind the wheel of the Jeep Cherokee. She smiled at him and said, "I don't believe in coincidences, Kamal."

"Neither do I," he said returning the smile. "I left Jerome at Port Authority and he bugged out on me. I wanted to touch base with you and didn't want to be seen entering your flat just now."

"I feel like a pariah," she said miserably.

"Oh, stop feeling sorry for yourself. You know I've got your back, but I'm no good to you locked up in some room with Conlan."

"What an asshole."

"You have a gift for understatement."

"So, what now?"

"Now we wait."

"Do you think he'll call?"

"You don't really know, do you?"

"Know what?" she asked.

"That he's crazy about you, that's what."

"I thought he was just crazy," she said giggling.

"That, too, but aren't we all."

"Hamm wanted to wash away his existence from me."

"What, the whole enchilada?"

"With guacamole, my Greek friend. He wanted to erase my knowledge of D-9 and Jerome along with it."

"You love him, don't you?" asked Kamal seriously.

"Of, course, but I wasn't sure it showed."

"You're still talking about him and what Hamm planned. Obviously, you didn't go along with it, so the logical conclusion is?"

"That I love him."

"Bingo. Will you go to him if he asks you?"

"What do you think?" she asked rhetorically.

"I think that I'm your ride."

"I love you, too, Kamal."

"I know. Right back at ya', Cookie."

"My phone is probably bugged."

"No, your phone is definitely bugged. So is mine, at least my land line."

"So how will he call?"

"One of the throw aways, I guess. He gave one to Watson, maybe he left one for you."

"That's a pretty expensive way to keep in touch, don't you think?" she said.

"He'll think of something better. Maybe Skype or something."

"Skype isn't private, Kamal."

"I know, but from a mobile device, who cares. He can bankrupt the NSA trying to chase him around, and if they finally do catch up to him, he just blinks out on them."

"God, I hope not. Hamm says it's ruining his insides. Mine, too."

"You're done with it, aren't you, Cookie?"

"Of course."

"Do you promise me?"

"I never make a promise I won't keep."

"That's not an answer, Cookie."

"No, it's not."

~

Jerome checked into a Hilton Hotel in Bar Harbor, Maine. He used cash for a three night stay and the name Henry Jacobs for the register. He settled into his room with a bucket of ice and a bottle of Dewar's scotch to wash down the long train ride from Newark, New Jersey. He had taken a bus from Port Authority to Newark right after Kamal had dropped him off. He was sorry for deceiving his good friend, but he needed to cut ties with the people of the city for a while. He felt like he was contaminating them with his presence and the NSA agents who were dogging him. He knew they would have the phones tapped, despite the repeal of the Patriot Act about to take effect in just two days. The wiretaps were in place for the time being, and he needed a work-around to maintain contact with Cookie. He missed her terribly and began to work out a plan to design a code. He reasoned that as long as both parties used the same primer, a code could be designed that would reduce a conversation to a series of numbers. It was really quite simple, and he had read about similar codes in a number of books. Conan Doyle's Sherlock Holmes was one of them. In the case of that story, the primer was an almanac. This time, it might be something as universal as the Bible. The series of numbers would correspond to page numbers, paragraph numbers, columns and a revolving system tied to specific dates and hours. A computer application would do all the legwork, once he could write the program and reduce it down to a flash drive. Then it would just be a matter of delivering the flash drive to Cookie, Kamal and Jerry Hamm. When the program is downloaded into a PC or a smart-phone, iPad or Mac, it would convert the seemingly random series of numbers into text. Child's play, actually. He was only sorry he couldn't see the look on Conlan's face when he realizes how easily his surveillance methods can be undermined. He decided to call it the Premier Primer. There were so many names in the first book of The New Testament, he would be sure to find numerous locations to identify specific letters for the code. At first he was concerned that the letter Q might present a problem due to its scarcity. When he did a search of The Book of Genesis, he found that it appeared no less than thirty-six times. All of those instances would be used in the primer on a rotating, random basis. Unless the primer was known, the code was literally unbreakable. When he did a search for the letter E, he found no less than 21,742 occurrences. That is 21,742 different locations in the primer for only one of the twenty-six letters in the English alphabet. When used on a rotating random basis, the permutations were mind-boggling.

~

Jerome purchased four small flash-drives into which he loaded the primer. Then it was a matter of delivery. He decided the best way was to place them in an overnight delivery envelope and mail them to Jerry Hamm's apartment. The NSA had limitless power to violate the rights of the general public with wiretaps, listening devices, vehicle tracking transmitters and surveillance cameras, but thankfully, the United States Postal System remained beyond their reach. The outside of the envelope mailed to Hamm was labeled, *Patient Records, Extremely Confidential! For the Eyes of Dr. Jerry Hamm Only!* When Hamm received the package, he knew instantly what it contained. He placed one of the flash-drives into his laptop recorder and received the message: *Download Me, Jerry, and then incinerate immediately.* When he did so and opened the introduction file, he was given instructions to deliver the remaining three flash-drives to Kamal Stanos, Woodhouse Watson and Cookie Doe. Each had a personal message along with instruction on how to use the primer. This resulted in a communication network that would remain outside the auspices of the government agencies who might like to monitor them. The urgency of confidentiality was stressed with the understanding that discovery might lead to an extended stay at the facilities located at Guantanamo Bay, Cuba. Not a very nice place to vacation for the most part. The spooks were so terrorist crazy after 911, and rightly so for the most part, that it was extremely important not to resemble a cell. *Just because they're paranoid, doesn't mean they're not after you.* A healthy dose of paranoia was a very useful device for the acquaintances of Dr. Jerome Cleveland.

~

Cookie received her first email from Jerome shortly after she downloaded the primer into her laptop computer. It was essentially a love letter, although it looked a lot like this:

5462726*404 674 648..54/

65216746554016504654601506640*046051065046501**4551068/650191550959590498831367450759451059450888.164664016640000004000446604660467841*80779501**57855578488454919540954095700094504950494095089852913934912942902909219290920914294949580859450150945097495089507950*18*/1207495019501*084*81200195409510*84*80*081*8*69510591519*7**8**788540196504**81018*8470*88524*8021*8400458*8401*180*45808*810*810*8084757868526501819*8014 0845958986862868298785549 *757079509750114//40479748049504194759974/*480944097087*084*945945078958/098/5208/96580498*804940919154798750981*842*78*787*8*/56546551024914094501650495140049*50419150*74*804975097840*85705740*8570*58409570*845097509450*78/*8491212942298249821495102676514009570954929450795049509795849059750954929450975 0495

65216746554016504654609150 6640*046051065046501**45510658/6501915509595 9049883136745075945105945088 88.16466401664000000040000446604660467841*80779501**5785557848845491954095409570009450495049409508985291393491294290290921929092091429494958085945015094509749508950 7950*18*/1207495019501*084*81200195409510*84*80*081*8*69510591519*7**8**788540196504**81018*8470*88524*8021*8400458*8401*180*45808*810*810*8084757868526501819*8014 0845958986862868298785549 *757079509750114//4047974 8049504194759974/*480944097087*084*945945078958/098/

146

5208/96580498*80494091915479875o981*842*78*787*8*/565465

5102491409450165049514oo49*50419150*74*8o4975097840*857o

5740*857o*58409570*845097509450*78/*84912129422982498214

55106508/65o191550

9595904988313674507594510594508888.164664o1664000000400

0446604660467841*80779501**5785557848845491954095409570

009450495049409508985291393491294290290921929092091429

494958085945015094509749508950795o*18*/1207495o19501*o84

*81200195409510*84*8o*o81*8*6951o591519*7**8**78854o1965o

4**81o18*8470*88524*8o21*8400458*84o1*18o*45808*81o*81o*

8o84757868526501819*8o14084595898686286829878549

*757079509750114//4047974

8o49504194759974/*480944097087*o84*945945078958/o98/

5208/96580498*80494091915479875o981*842*78*787*8*/565465

51024914094501650496514oo4

546579*145465049841046950494094999842182498219820

4791298274

5784 5496 69124 549512

The actual text read:

Dearest Cookie,

How can I find the words to tell you how many regrets are in a circular dance around my sorry head? No man has the right to infect such a beautiful existence as you have every right to enjoy. If I could turn back time, I would do so only for the purpose of erasing my inclusion into your precious life. I pray for a lifetime to make it up to you. I will become a better man if only for the purpose of righting the wrongs I have inflicted upon your wonderful soul.

My nights are troubled, which I know is a circumstance of my own design, and I deserve no better because of the ills I have orchestrated with my shortcomings. I want to cover your lovely, physical chalice with kisses and apologies into the night and to the morning of our healing hearts. I will be the one you need to share your life with if you will just give me the chance to love you with my mind, body and soul.

Forever yours, Jerome

~

The message to Kamal was somewhat less romantic:

Kamal, My Good Friend,

I'm in a Hilton Hotel in Bar Harbor, Maine, for the next two days. After that, I plan to search the real estate market for a small house on the coastline north of here. I can't tell you where because I don't yet know myself where my travels will take me. I'll rent a car for the time being with a false named, although legitimate, credit card that I was able to purchase when I was in the city. The name on it is Henry Jacobs. It is the same name I used to check in here at the Hilton in case you need to contact me in an emergency. My room number is 419. For any non-emergency contact, please use the primer to create your messages via email. It is absolutely unbreakable, and as soon as Conlan realizes the futility of trying, he is likely to leave us all alone. You have the throw-away phones that I supplied, but please refrain from their use unless absolutely necessary. Then, dispose of them accordingly. I know I can always escape capture by going to D-9, but until I can get the gastro-intestinal problem solved, I am reluctant to go there. Take care, buddy. If you need anything from me like cash to work with, just shoot me a message and I'll supply you with a numbered account in Switzerland. Give my best to Watson and Art when you see them. I've sent them flash drives as well by way of Jerry Hamm in case they need to contact you or me. Be safe, we'll talk soon, Jerome.

~

Hamm's first message to Jerome read like this:

Dear Jerome,

I have unfortunate news. Your lovely friend Ms. Doe remains at risk because she refused to go along with erasure therapy. It involved the use of mild psychotropic drugs, but I don't believe that was her objection. It appears that her attraction to you is stronger than her wish for a healthy existence. She's pretty far gone, my friend. I don't know what you have, but you should bottle it and sell it. It's probably the syndrome of *I know I can save that sorry soul* effect. In any case, you might as well take out a gun and shoot the poor girl. Eventually, she is going to make the connection back to D-9 and her G.I. system may not handle it. If you care for the girl, save her life, Jerome. Break off your relationship as soon as you can. Give me the chance to heal her on this end.

Regards, Jerry

~

Cookie's first message was as follows:

How dare you?

You are a sorry excuse for a human being. You bet I'll give you the chance to make it up to me. I'll give you about fifty years to do so. You're going to be a very busy boy. How dare you let me fall in love with you and then bug out on me? That's right, I love you. I'm not sure why, though. You're not particularly attractive, and your laundry could use a good cleaning now and then. What a wild ride you took me on falling in and out of my universe. Thanks a lot for that. Now I'm stuck with a guy who is unstuck to his strings. I'm in love with a lamebrain who can't stay on his own brane. Way to go, Jerome. Why couldn't you just do something normal with your intellect. You could have been a nice nuclear physicist or an astronomer, but no . . . not Jerome Freaking Cleveland. *I have to make the world unsafe for all of mankind.* Sheese, can I pick 'em. You better tell me where you're hiding because I'm coming to get you, you sorry excuse of a transparent lover. And when I get there, you better have a necktie to hang on the door.

Yours extremely pissed, Cookie

Chapter Twenty

Jerome's next message to Cookie:

Not particularly good looking? Well considering you look like Peppermint Patty, I guess you would prefer someone who looks like Charlie Brown. Seriously, with your round face and all those freckles, when you first told me your name was Cookie, the first thing I thought of was oatmeal raisin. But I should tell you that oatmeal raisin is my favorite Cookie.

This form of correspondence is fine for two people merely needing to exchange information, but we're gone way past that at this point. We need to talk. Call me on one of the throwaways. I'm at the Bar Harbor Hilton Hotel, room four-nineteen. I got a message from Jerry Hamm that you're not cooperating with his erasure therapy. That is not an option. I'm standing by in my room until your call. Make it now, Cookie.

Love, Jerome

~

Jerome picked up on the first ring. "I miss you."

"I miss you, too, Jerome, but what makes you think you can tell me what to do?" asked Cookie hotly.

"Someone has to have the sense to turn away from D-9," said Jerome.

"D-9? Who the fuck cares about D-9, you big jerk? It's *you* I care about, Jerome. Hamm told me that I'll lose any memory of you if I complete the erasure therapy. Is that what you really want?" she asked urgently.

"Yes, Cookie. It's too dangerous to go on the way we are now. Our hearts will find each other again if you have faith."

"Faith? What the hell are you talking about? I've waited my whole life to find someone who I care about, and now you want me to throw it all away because you don't think I can control myself not to wink out to another dimension. Do you know how stupid that sounds?"

"I'm sorry, Cookie. There's nothing else that makes any sense. You have to go along with the therapy. We have to do it one at a time. I'll undergo the erasure after I get settled and re-establish contact with you. It will give me a chance to sweep you off of your feet all over again."

"I'll sweep you, you transparent twerp. Nothing doing. I'm coming up to Maine to kick your sorry ass."

"No, Cookie, that's exactly what you can't do right now. You'll lead the spooks right to my door. If you love me, just trust me. Let Hamm do the therapy and I'll find you again. I'll make you fall in love with me again. You have to trust me, Cookie."

"Alright, Jerome. I trust you, but there's something I have to do before I let Hamm scramble my brains."

"What? What are you talking about? What do you have to do?"

"It's Roadie. He's gone missing."

"What are you saying?" asked Jerome.

"Art said he darted out into the street on 34th. He was avoiding a car coming at him and he just disappeared. Art can't find him, and we both think we know where he went."

"You're not going back to D-9, Cookie. I forbid it. I won't stand for it, you foolish girl," said Jerome with fire in his voice.

"You started all this crap, Jerome. I'm just cleaning up your mess."

"But even if you find Roadie, how the hell are you going to teach him to make the transfer by himself?"

"I'm going to teach him how to bark."

"Did you just say what I think you did?"

"Oh, yes, Jerome. It just gets weirder and weirder down in this rabbit hole of yours. Apparently, Roadie is not a barker. He never barks according to Art the gypsy. Now he's going to learn while he's learning something else that will bring his strings back to this brane. Wish me luck, Jerome. I'm late, I'm late, for a very important date," said Cookie as she broke the connection.

Jerome was helpless to do anything to stop Cookie from so very far away. He sadly said, "Good luck," into an empty phone line.

~

Cookie met Art the gypsy juggler in front of The Empire State Building on 34th street. He held his arms out and gave her a big hug saying, "I love you, Cookie. You know you don't have to do this," being well aware of the danger to her the transfer would mean. Art knew that traveling to D-9 wreaked havoc on her G.I. system and that she was taking a big risk without any assurances that she could be successful in retrieving the dog. All she said was, "Yes, I do, Art. Roadie's there because of me. Don't worry. I'll get him back."

Cookie looked around for a suitable place to make the transfer. She mused to herself; *At least Superman had phone booths.* She ducked into a nearby doorway, and an instant later, she was gone. The first thing she noticed was the rain. She had materialized into a fierce downpour, and despite the warm August temperature, she felt instantly cold and wet. She looked around her for any sight of Roadie and came up empty. The next thing she noticed was the lack of sound. For some reason, she was monitoring D-9 without entirely experiencing it. She could see masses of people going in and coming out of the huge building, but could hear no sounds of the city whatsoever. She knew that Roadie was experiencing the same thing. She decided to call out to him, "ROADIE! WHERE ARE YOU? HERE, ROADIE! COME TO YOUR AUNT COOKIE, BUDDY! COME ON, ROADIE, IT'S TIME TO GO HOME! ROOOAAADDIIEEEE!!!!!!"

Still nothing. There was no sign of the dog.

~

Kamal sent a message to Jerome using the Premier Code with his laptop:

Jerome,

I just heard the news from Dr. Hamm. Cookie's crazy for walking out of his office like that. I'm blaming you, too. You got her into this mess in the first place and then you just cut and run to Maine? Jesus, man, if you're not going to stand beside her, at least try to convince her what a schlemiel you are, and cut her loose. She can do a lot better. Now I hear she's going after Art's dog in D-9. How does that make you feel? Seriously, dude, you might have retrieved your intellect from D-9, but maybe you left something else back there. Your heart, man.

Kamal

~

Jerome sent a return to Kamal's message:

Kamal,

Do you suppose you could cut me some slack? I know I'm poison for Cookie, I told her so. I never asked her to fall for me, and I didn't want to fall for her. Sometimes we don't have control over our hearts, buddy. Right now I could use a friend instead of a critic. Cookie needs you as well. You know she's gone to D-9 down on 34th street near the Empire State Building. When she finds the dog, she's going to need a place to make the transfer back unobserved. Maybe you can help. Did you ever think of that? If you really are her friend, maybe you could circle the block in the Jeep to give her a way to materialize without drawing attention to herself. If you need a different car, just buy it. Charge it to me with the credit card I left in

155

your apartment. By the time the spooks catch on, I'm hoping that Cookie will be out of there before the shit hits the fan. You can do it, Kamal. Do it for Cookie. Or else, do it for me and I'll owe you another one. I know, the meter is still running.

Jerome

~

When Cookie spotted Roadie, she didn't recognize him at first. He looked like a large rat. His fur was soaked to the skin and discolored by the sooty, city streets of downtown. He ran to her open arms, tail wagging a mile a minute and what looked like a definite smile on his face. He grabbed him up and said, "Roadie, you're a mess! But you are a sight for sore eyes. I've missed you. How did you get here? Do you know how you got here, boy?"

Roadie said nothing. Roadie always said nothing. He was not a barker according to Art the gypsy. That was about to change. Cookie said to him, "Roadie, I want you to speak." Roadie said nothing. "Come on, Roadie, you can do it, speak!" Roadie said nothing.

~

Kamal was circling the block in the Jeep Cherokee. He figured that Conlan had no idea that Cookie was downtown trying to retrieve the dog. He knew he had a good hour before anyone might notice a familiar car circling the block. The downtown traffic was heavy, and Kamal knew all the tricks to slip into loading zones and double park to kill time and stay in the area. He knew from Art that she made the transfer from the front of the building, so he did most of his stalling tactics there. After about forty minutes, he finally hit pay dirt in the form of a sharp sound from the back seat of the car. It was a dog's bark right in his ear. The loud noise was very startling, but nevertheless a very musical sound. He knew what it meant. Roadie and Cookie were back. Both of them were soaked to the skin and smelled like wet dog, but they were beautiful. Kamal took off in search of Art the gypsy juggler who was last seen circling the block on foot. When Art saw the Jeep, he jogged over and jumped in the back seat with Cookie and his prodigal dog. He gave the dog a big kiss on the lips and then did the same to Cookie. She told him, "That could have been more hygienic, Art. Now I'll bet my breath will smell like Milk Bones," she said laughing.

"On you it smells marvelous," said Art. "Cookie, you're the best, you know that?"

"I know, Art. I know now that I'm the best, but soon, I may have to learn it all over again."

Art knew what she was talking about, as did Kamal. He expressed both of their feelings when he said, "We're here for you, Cookie. That's one thing that will never change regardless of how it goes in Hamm's office."

"I know," said Cookie. "I love you guys."

They both said together, "Right back at ya,"

Roadie said, "Arf!"

~

157

Cookie began the erasure therapy the next day. The first session was in Hamm's office and then the remaining sessions of the next five weeks took place in his apartment. He was supposed to be resting after his ordeal of the taxi accident and his subsequent surgical procedure to remove the glass pieces from his cerebral cortex. His good friend, Helmut Burger dropped in on him from time to time to play chess. Once he scolded Dr. Hamm when Cookie showed up for one of her sessions. He told him, "Jerry, you are a very *bad boy.*"

"I know, Helmut," said Hamm, "but it is for a very *good cause.*"

After three weeks of treatment, more than twelve sessions, Cookie was finally unable to recall any suggestion of instability with respect to a slippage back into D-9. Then after two more weeks, she finally lost all memory of Jerome Cleveland. Dr. Hamm was able to plant suggestions in her mind that would lead her to have some semblance of curiosity about a man named Henry Jacobs who lived in an oceanfront cottage in Maine. He told her that the vistas were beautiful there and conducive to an artistic talent that she had apparently turned her back on. Hamm told her that her agent was anxious for her to get back to work because her public expressed an outcry for more of her oil paintings. Cookie wasn't able to remember actually painting landscapes at all, but her interest was growing by the day. She found herself doodling on a sketch pad during a few of the last sessions she had with Dr. Hamm.

~

Chapter Twenty-one

At the corner of 47th Street and The Avenue of the Americas, a large granite building was the property of the United States Government. The sixth floor was the domain of the National Security Agency Field Office also known as *Ground Zero Plus Six*. Agent William Conlan had the ignominious distinction of being the unfortunate recipient of a six word voice mail message that was the worst nightmare of any field operative. The emotionless female voice stated merely, "Your presence is requested at six."

Nothing more was needed. The implications spoke volumes. The phrase, *requested at six* could only mean one thing. Whether you worked for the Federal Bureau of Investigation located on the fifth floor, or the Central Intelligence Agency on the third floor, or the National Security Agency on the sixth floor, *at six* was the designated phrase for the building that held the administrative offices that no field operative had any business visiting unless . . . you were being called on the carpet.

Agent Jeremy Arnold was sitting in the driver's seat of the Crown Victoria outside the building with a serious expression on his face and a good deal of perspiration saturating his white shirt and shoulder harness securing his Glock. He wisely chose not to wear his jacket. Sitting next to him was Agent Conlan wiping his brow with the sleeve of his sports coat. He turned to Arnold and said to him,

"They say it's a long ride up, Jeremy. The longest six floors you ever ride."

"It may not be with prejudice, Bill."

"Thanks for the thought, but we're all grown-ups at this party."

"Good luck, Sir," he said finally.

"It's been a pleasure riding with you, Jeremy."

"Bill," was all Agent Arnold said in parting shaking his hand.

Conlan exited the Crown Victoria, and then with two hands, he gently pressed the passenger door closed with a soft *snick*. As he walked through the front door of the building, he watched Agent Arnold pull away from the curb.

The woman seated at the reception desk on the sixth floor greeted him with the cold efficiency of a funeral director, "Your shield and your weapon remain here, Agent Conlan."

"Naturally," said Conlan. "Wouldn't want me to shoot back."

"Relax, Mr. Conlan. I've been instructed to return them to you when you leave."

Well, at least that's something of a consolation he thought. *Maybe the director will let me make my case . . . but of course, that was a pipe dream at best. The director didn't have time to meet with field agents unless . . .*

"Come in," came the answer to his knock on the door.

Seated at a large mahogany desk was the Director of the National Security Agency. He had only two men ranked above him within the entire network of the United States Government. The first was the Secretary of Homeland Security, and the second was the President. His corner office, featuring two large picture windows overlooking the city below, was the consummate metaphor for his position of absolute power. If God himself were seeking a promotion, he might do well to approach this man. Conlan was surprised by his understated attire, although he thought he understood the reason for it. The director wore a raspberry, cashmere sweater over his blue, cotton, button-downed oxford shirt. He wore no tie or jacket, and his legs beneath his khaki colored slacks were crossed revealing a worn pair of loafers and no socks. He addressed Agent Conlan with a curious air of familiarity. "Bill, I'm glad you could come. Please have a seat. I'm expecting a call shortly that I think you might like to hear."

A Call? wondered Conlan. *What kind of call could the director be expecting that he would want me to be privy to? Don't tell me it's the President,* his fears were quickly rising to the surface of his mind.

Just then, the speakerphone on the desk came to life, "Director Ford, I have Senator Blake on the line," said the woman who had taken his weapon and shield a few minutes earlier.

"Thank you, Denise, please put him through," said the director. "Senator Blake," he spoke loudly into the speakerphone, "to what do I owe the pleasure of this phone call?"

"Did you forget my first name, John? Oh, I get it, you're not alone," said the senator. "Well, let's just forget all about my supposition that you have company since I never made this call in the first place, if you get my drift."

"Drift received loud and clear, Sir. How can I be of assistance?"

"How indeed, John? Do you remember my niece?"

"How could I forget her, Ed? She's a gem. Did you know she sent me a case of scotch for my last birthday?"

"That sounds like her. Was it good scotch?" asked Senator Blake.

"She knows my favorite, Ed."

"That's nice, John. Listen, I'm going to give you the chance to return the favor."

"Oh?" asked the director raising his eyebrows at Agent Conlan, knowing full-well what was coming.

"Oh, indeed," said the senator with some edge of menace in his voice. "I was sorry to learn that he is one of yours, John."

"I nipped it in the bud as soon as I learned about it, Ed."

"I'm glad to hear that. Cookie will be glad as well."

"Tell her that I think about her every time I eat pancakes, Ed."

"I'll do that," said the senator hanging up the line.

Director Ford had enjoyed his conversation with Senator Blake even though he was figuratively lying on the floor with a foot on his neck. He knew the senator was enjoying it as well. He liked to chastise his good friend John Ford every chance he got to make up for his inferior golf game. He was confident that the phone call would result in at least three strokes during their next outing at Congressional National Golf Links in Bethesda, Maryland.

The director asked Agent Conlan, "You know who that was on the phone, don't you Bill?"

"Senator Blake from the great state of New York," said Conlan.

"And do you know who his niece is, Bill?"

"I do now," said Conlan.

"Well, here's what you may not know," began Ford, "her mother's maiden name was Catherine T. Blake until she married John J. Doe of Doe Industries. She was Catherine T. Blake of the Vermont timberland Blakes. She bought her brother Edward a senate seat for his thirty-ninth birthday. He's enjoyed that seat uncontested for over twenty-five years. Now, when his sister Catherine passed away, do you think she left her daughter Jane merely a syrup company?"

"Jane?" asked Conlan.

"It's the name on her birth certificate. It would be on her driver's license as well if she had one," said Ford.

"What kind of kid doesn't get her driver's license?" asked Conlan.

"A city kid, William. She's never needed one. She's had her own personal chauffer since she was ten years old. Now you realize the kind of people you've been pissing on."

"Yes, Sir," said Conlan turning color.

"I understand Ms. Doe is now in therapy. It's rumored she had been suffering memory loss as well. Do I have to say it?" asked the director.

"No, Sir," said Conlan looking down at his shoes.

"You're right, but I'm going to say it anyway. Edward Blake sits on the Homeland Security Means Committee that funds the chair sitting underneath my tail that is currently between my legs. I don't like it when my tail is between my legs, William. If I'm not mistaken, you are about six months out from receiving your pension and living a life of luxury on some God-damned fishing boat somewhere in

Florida at the expense of the good old U.S. of A. And who do you think you have to thank for that fortunate circumstance?"

"Understood, Sir. It won't happen again, Sir, I assure you."

"You bet your ass it won't. Now get out," he said hotly.

"Thank you, Sir," was all that Agent Conlan could think to say. Director Ford had said enough and just waved his hand at the door for Conlan to leave his office.

When the secretary at the desk on the way out handed him back his shield and gun, she told him, "Have a nice day."

"A little late for that," said Conlan heading for the elevator.

~

Five weeks later, Jerome had agreed to travel back to the city for his erasure therapy sessions in Jerry Hamm's office. On the way in for his first session, he noticed Cookie sitting on a chair in the waiting room. She had been called back into Hamm's office for a post-therapy support session to reinforce the hypnotic suggestions to surrender any knowledge of either D-9 or Jerome Cleveland. Jerome smiled at her, and she smiled back at him. "I'm Cookie," she offered introducing herself.

"I'm pleased to meet you," said Jerome. "My name is Henry Jacobs."

Just then, Dr. Hamm entered the waiting room and said, "Oh, Mr. Jacobs, I'm glad you're here. This is the young gentleman I was telling you about, Cookie. I was thinking you'll find that you have a lot in common."

"Oh?" asked Jerome. "Are you interested in traveling, Cookie?"

"Yes," she said, "as a matter of fact I am."

"Maybe we could meet for some coffee sometime and talk about it," said Jerome.

"Maybe we can," said Cookie. "I'll be free later today. Would that work for you, Mr. Jacobs?"

"Absolutely," he said smiling. "And it's Henry."

As she was leaving, Hamm opened the door to his treatment room and said to Jerome, "You're making the right decision, Jerome. I know you won't be sorry."

"I know I won't, Jerry. But just don't forget to remind me I have a date for coffee."

"I won't forget, Jerome. "By the way, do you know what day it is?" he asked.

"Why, of course," said Jerome. "It's Thursday."

"And how do you *feel* about Thursday?" asked Hamm.

Thinking of his coffee date with Cookie he answered, "I'm not really sure, but I think it may become my favorite day."

~~~

www.ingramcontent.com/pod-product-compliance
Lightning Source LLC
Chambersburg PA
CBHW070327130626
46556CB00007B/2757

9 780099 664870 7